BEFORE SHE WAS MINE

BEFORE SHE WAS MINE

AMELIA WILDE

Cover Design: Coverlüv

Cover Model: Alex Perez

Photographer: Eric David Battershell Photography

For my husband

1

DAYTON

MY MISSING FOOT hurts like a bitch.

You've probably heard of phantom pain, and I'll tell you right now—you're picturing it wrong. It's not nebulous, an aching vapor in roughly the size and shape of the limb you've lost—in my case, my left leg, starting just below the knee.

There is no shin. There is no foot. There are no toes.

They were irreparably mangled at the base of a mountain in Afghanistan, and it's almost definitely my fault.

But fault has nothing to do with the very real burn at the back of my missing heel, like I shoved my feet into running shoes like a lazy bastard, not bothering to stick a finger between my ankle and the heel tab until I'm several miles in and it's already too late. Fault has nothing to do with the sharp pebble between my second and third toes, driving into the webbing with every step I take along the filthy snowstreaked steps, or the burning stretch in my arch threatening to root in my heel. If that happens, I'm fucked, because there's no cure for a bum heel in a foot that doesn't exist.

The phantom pain rubs shoulders with the real pain where what's left of my leg—what the doctors call *residual limb* like it's the dry end of a party sub—and *that* pain, at least, I can take full credit for.

Ten steps away from the exit of the 50th Street subway, it's already throbbing from standing on the train. The stairs are too narrow. It should be better on solid ground. The lady ahead of me on the steps doesn't know that. The handle of her purse slips down her shoulder, inch by inch, the top partially unzipped. She curls her head toward her shoulder but it doesn't do anything to pin down the strap. Whatever's in the cardboard box is either fragile or too heavy to hold with one hand.

"Shit," she whispers.

I step up beside her, the extra effort of catching up putting more pressure on the missing foot. My arch twists, pulls. It's the only way to keep going, and I have to keep going. The exit beckons. I want to accept the invitation. I'm not a fucking hero, but I'm not a total asshole, either. I want to ignore her. I don't.

"Give you a hand with that box?"

She flicks her eyes over to me. "I'm okay."

"You're about to lose half your purse."

One more glance. The dress pants must help my case. "If you're sure—"

I take the box and she hitches up the purse strap on her

shoulder. Without the added weight she springs up the steps, waiting for me at the top. It's *heavy.* It's a good counterbalance for my shitty prosthetic but it makes my stump press into the socket, setting the hot spots on fire.

Out on the sidewalk I tip it back into her hands. "What do you have in there?"

A rueful shake of her head. "Books. I couldn't let them go." She turns away and back again. "Thanks."

It's three and a half blocks to where I'm going and cold as hell even though it's sunny. The sidewalks are a mix of sand and slush and petrified dog shit and that *pain* between my toes. If I didn't know better, I'd take off my boot and look for that pebble, rub at the arch.

No, I wouldn't. Not with the buildings huddling together above me, blank windows watching my sorry progress. I should have canceled this meeting.

The foot that isn't there presses down through a gray layer of slush and jerks sideways. I curse under my breath. I wore work boots today. I shouldn't have worn work boots, but it's this kind of weather that makes me glad I stuffed my metal replacement foot into something sturdy, with waterproof canvas. Even the thick treads aren't a match for the endless winter nightmare in Manhattan.

This is a waste of time. Things were going fine at the factory in Queens. Totally fucking fine, except for the muscle spasms that knocked me off balance when I lifted the assembled windows onto the racks, or the way my hands swelled for days on end from the chemical baths if I worked Section 12.

If I'd had some painkillers, it would've been good, but that asshole O'Connors at the VA had gone so far as to put down his clipboard and look me in the eye at my appointment last week, as if he was a wise old general and not a green doctor younger than I am.

You can't keep putting your body through this punishment. That's what he said *to me.* As if I deserve anything less than a punishing job—than mindless, manual labor.

Shit. Did I miss the building?

I shuffle myself over to a wrought-iron fence planted in the concrete and lean my hip against it. There's not much slush here. I dig into the pocket of my dress pants, bought new at the last minute.

I have a card.

It reads:

Heroes on the Homefront

Veteran Services

540 W. 50th Street

New York, NY 10019

The sight of it makes both my feet itch. If I still had both of them, instead of dragging around this titanium-alloy bull-shit, I'd run back to the train station right now.

Too late for that. I'm already in front of 540 W. 50th, and there are giant windows up front. They've been cleaned recently, so I have a full unobstructed view of the reception-ist, who smiles at me and gives me a little wave.

Jesus Christ.

The socket on the temp prosthetic is digging into my leg somehow, sending sharp sparks of pain up into my thigh. The gel liner that's supposed to protect it is worn down. I reach for the door and my leg resists picking up my foot. I swing it twice to get myself through, and on the second swing my boot catches in a snowdrift a few inches from the door, which throws me off balance.

I'll never let them see my shame. Heroes on the Homefront —what utter bullshit. I'm not a hero. I can't even get through the front door without everybody in here—some woman has now joined the receptionist behind the desk, absolutely wonderful—giving me pitying looks.

I let the door swing shut behind me and step fully into the lobby. The receptionist is half out of her seat as if she's about to rush over and take my arm, and Christ, if she does that, I'm done with this place and every other place, to be honest. She must see it in my face because she sits down, still wearing the encouraging smile that's making my gut twist, and watches me approach the desk, eyes wide and shining.

"Welcome to Heroes on the Homefront," she says, big brown eyes practically glistening now, for fuck's sake. "How can I help you today?"

"Dayton Nash. I have an appointment at eleven."

She nods as if she's in the presence of greatness—I'm going to die of disgust—and picks up the handset of her phone. The other woman disappears in a flash of bleach-blonde pixie cut. "Have a seat, Mr. Nash. There's coffee and tea, if you're interested." Ms. Pitying Receptionist lifts her chin toward a coffee cart over by the opposite window. As if I'm going to drag myself all the way across the room while she watches her own personal performance of a *hero on the homefront.* I take the nearest seat.

And wait.

Five minutes tick by, then ten, then fifteen. It's ten past now, and too hot in the waiting room. Too boring. The sleek furniture is fine for five minutes but not for twenty, and the music—god, the music, it's soft country and right now I can't stand it. I can't stand the framed photos of the American flag on the walls. I can't stand the black carpeting, shot through with red and white and blue. And I *can't* fucking stand that I'm here in the first place like some asshole who can't get a job on his own, who thinks he *deserves* something cushy, something pre-arranged. If only that cow-eyed receptionist knew what I've done. What I still could do, if push came to shove. The ends justify the means.

Twenty-two minutes.

It shouldn't be this hard to do the shit you're supposed to do. To work a job on the right side of the law. To claw yourself out of the black, numb despair that creeps into your chest at night, that makes you get a cramp in the foot that doesn't exist, a cramp that won't release its grip until the sun comes up and you have to be on the factory floor, making windows for buildings you'll never see.

I'm leaving.

It's not worth it. It's not worth *this.*

I shift my weight forward in this hellish, stylish seat.

"Mr. Nash?"

It's not the receptionist's voice. It's not a voice I've heard in a long time, and at the sound of it my toes—real *and* imagined —curl. Pleasure or shame? I don't know.

I drag my eyes away from the carpet and shove myself up out of the chair as some other guy makes his way past. I don't let myself look until I'm upright in case it's not her, in case it's a hallucination I'd be better off ignoring.

It's not a hallucination.

It's really her.

A different version of her. A gorgeous, grown-up version of her. Not the gritted-teeth version going too fast down Suicide Hill, snow and determination in her eyes, or the tomato-red mortified version standing alone at the corner of the school dance, but I'd know her anywhere.

Anywhere is *here*. Right in front of me, saying my name.

The strangest desire wraps its fists around my heart and squeezes. I wonder if her hair still smells like Pantene.

My foot doesn't hurt at all.

2

SUMMER

His eyes give him away.

He's backlit by unearthly winter light from the huge front windows, his face in shadow, but those *eyes*. It doesn't matter that we're standing in the sleek, subtly patriotic waiting room at Heroes on the Homefront, where professionalism and empathy are our top priorities. Every inch of me is alive with his presence.

It's Dayton. *My* Dayton. Or—Wes's Dayton, really. He was never *mine*.

That doesn't matter. I'd know those eyes anywhere.

I dismissed it when I saw the name on my appointment list. D. Nash could've been anyone. No reason to get nervous. No reason to think he'd walk into this office in Midtown, three months after I started my dream job. To keep the workload under control, we don't do verifications or research until the veterans have attended an intake meeting. About a quarter of the people on my list every day don't show up.

Dayton showed up.

So did my last appointment, which is why I'm late for Dayton. Gregory DeWitt looked fine, sitting in the waiting room, even flashed me a smile on the way back to my office. I thought it'd be simple. A little brush-up of the resume, a few questions about his general interests, and I could look at listings before my eleven o'clock.

He wasn't fine.

He'd sweat through his shirt by the time he sat in the chair across from me and said *listen, I don't go out much*. By "much" he meant that he hadn't left his apartment in three weeks, but he was running out of money. The VA was dragging its feet on approving him for disability, one domino falling, then another. I couldn't kick him out. It wouldn't have been right.

I had the apology on my lips when I stepped into the waiting room but the words fall to the floor and scatter. I tuck my hands together to stop them from trembling.

Carla, the receptionist, is about to lose her mind. I can tell by the way she's sitting forward in her ergonomic desk chair, pretending not to notice that the silence between me and one Mr. Nash—Day—has gone on too long not to be awkward.

That's not good.

I look into those dark eyes, those wells of pain flecked with surprise, and forget to be professional.

He's *different*. Even broader than the last time I saw him, more muscled, and peeking out from beneath the collar of his shirt are the black curves of tattoos. The way he's standing isn't how I remember it, but he's been in the service. That changes a man. It's changed Dayton. The evidence is right in front of me.

Tattoos.

He never had tattoos before, and if I'm right, the lines I'm seeing are the tip of the iceberg. A wild curiosity ignites in the center of my chest, a dry brush going up at the strike of a match, clarifying my strange double vision. I see him as he is. I see him as he used to be. The two versions compete for my focus.

I move before I can stop myself, crossing to the first row of those godawful chairs. They look lovely. Try sitting in one for twenty minutes, though, and you'll change your opinion.

I shouldn't do this—it's against the code of *being in the office* —but every breath is tinged with a strange excitement, a strange dread. I can't help myself. I throw my arms around him, right above his waist, and hug the hard, solid mass of his body.

It's a mistake.

For an instant we're standing together, right there in the waiting room for everyone to see, and then my freak hug has knocked him off balance. He takes a step onto his left foot. Something's not right. He goes over, sitting down hard into the chair behind him.

"Shit."

"Oh—" I can't get my arms untangled from his waist fast enough, so I fall along with him, and both of us are tangled up in what has to be the greatest mortification the world has ever known. "I'm sorry, Day, I—" The old nickname swims up from years ago, from back when I could hear his low voice through the wall while he played video games with Wes in the middle of the night, and my face goes molten. I yank my hands from behind his back and straighten up.

Oh, God.

No, of *course* I'm not the little girl he knew back then. I'm all grown up and perfectly composed. I meant for this to happen.

"I'm so sorry," I say, feeling the weight of everyone's eyes against my skin. There are two other veterans in the waiting room, and then there's Carla. The wheel of her chair squeaks as she shifts her position, no doubt to get a better look.

"It's fine." His voice is gruff, and when he glances up I see something in his eyes that I missed before. It's gone so fast, locked down behind a tightening in his jaw, that maybe I'm wrong.

It looked like shame.

But for the life of me, I can't imagine what Day could be ashamed of. He's a hero.

I smooth my hair back into its ponytail. *Pretend he's like anyone else.* His coat, navy blue, over a white dress shirt. Tan dress pants, an adult version of the khakis he and Wes used to wear for special occasions.

The pants are hiked up to the socket of a prosthesis.

That explains why he lost his balance when I tackled him like a teenager at a One Direction concert.

I breathe away the heat pressing against my cheeks, but he's seen me looking. I offer him a hand up. It's the least I can do, even if the gesture is totally ineffectual. I'm not a weakling. He's tall and muscular, but I could at least—

He dismisses the offer with a shake of his head and pushes himself up using the arm of the chair instead. Day narrows his eyes over my shoulder—jeez, Carla, be a little less obvious, would you?—and looks down at me.

Take control of the situation. This is your job. You are here to help. To prove that you can help.

"Let's head back to my office."

I try for a neutral tone, like Dayton is any other client, but he's not any other client. He doesn't smile but the corner of his mouth lifts up a fraction of an inch.

"Okay."

How long has it been since I last saw him? Up until this moment, if you asked me, I'd have been able to give you an exact number of days. But right now, standing next to him in this waiting room, the cold, clean scent of him filling my lungs, I have no idea. Has it been three years? How did I ever go that long without seeing him? My soul is lit up like the Empire State Building on a clear night. My soul...and other parts of me. It's like my soul doesn't remember that he took my heart in those big, rough hands and squeezed until it broke.

"Summer?"

My name is soft on his lips, and watching those lips form the word sends illicit pleasure tumbling through my brain.

"Yeah?"

A nod of his head, a quick gesture behind me. "Your office?"

Now the blush takes over. I can't stop it. "Right. Of course. Right." I turn on my heel and lead the way.

3

SUMMER

Twelve Years Ago

Only people who really, *really* love winter would brave the top of Suicide Hill. The biggest hill. The *forbidden* hill behind the middle school.

I *love* winter.

My mom named me for the warmest season of the year, but give me inches of white snow any day.

It's not cool to hate summer vacation, and really, I don't. Every summer my dad takes three weeks off from his job at the plant, and since mom teaches seventh-grade English in the next town over, that leaves plenty of time to drive all the way from New York, where we live, to Michigan, where my Grandpa Louie bought two cottages on one long lot in the 1970s. When he died he gave one to my mom and one to my aunt Holly and every single summer we go on vacation with her, and her husband Tom and their three kids. I like the pontoon boat rides best.

They can't beat sledding.

Especially on snow days. Like today.

School's closed for us, but not mom, so she left Wes in charge. I don't need him to watch me. I'm eleven. I'm old enough to take care of myself. He's better at ordering pizza, I guess, which he promised to do when we're done sledding.

I'm not sure if we're going to be done anytime soon because when we got here, to the top of Suicide Hill, his best friend Dayton appeared out of nowhere. The woods, really, which isn't nowhere. I'm pretty sure he lives on the other side of those woods in the cul-de-sac my mom doesn't like to drive to. I heard her telling Dad the other night that she was going to be glad when Wes got his official license and she wouldn't have to drive Day home, but I bet she didn't mean it. It's just a cul-de-sac.

For a snow day, it's not very cold. School's closed but there are lots of other kids at Suicide because who could resist snow like this? Deep and fluffy and cushioning. It's perfect for sledding, and when Wes woke up at 11:15 I couldn't help asking him, and for once he didn't pretend he was too old for it.

So here I am, at the top of Suicide Hill with my bright orange saucer, waiting for the perfect opportunity.

We're not supposed to be here. Nobody's allowed during school hours because it's so steep, and there's a huge boulder at the bottom of the hill that's a memorial for a boy named Victor who died in 1991, according to the big metal plaque on the front of it. When we left the house Wes started walking here instead of the regular sledding hill at the park on Pine, but what was I going to say?

The rough edges of my hat, barely blunted by the fleece on the inside, rub against my cheeks and I scan the hill, clutching my saucer with my mittened hands. There's a group of boys from my grade here acting like maniacs. My heart is racing and I haven't even gone down yet. The thought that I'm going to—that I'm going to hop down onto the saucer on my knees and go screaming down the new snow—makes my arms tingle, same as when I sneak three more Oreos from the cupboard while Mom's watching. Two of the boys go down again, crashing into each other at the bottom of the hill, yelling at each other through laughter that the other one is an asshole.

Boys.

I roll my eyes and steal another glance over at Dayton and Wes, who are huddled close together. Wes has the blue saucer from the garage and Dayton doesn't have anything. Day's back is to me. The boys at the bottom of the hill don't have shoulders that broad, and even under his winter coat, I can tell that football practice is making him more muscular.

I wish he'd look at me.

I wish he'd do more than look at me, honestly, but I'm not sure what I'd want him to do. Up until this fall, I thought kissing was pretty weird and gross, but then my best friend Amy stole one of her mom's romance books and we read it under the covers one night when she stayed over. I couldn't picture most of what was going on—why do they write them like that?—but when we skipped to the part about the first kiss, it was Dayton's face that popped into mind.

So embarrassing.

He'd never want to kiss me. He's fourteen, a freshman in high school already, and I'm a seventh-grader. He plays on the football team.

One of the boys my age shoves the other and he falls backward into the snow. I try to picture kissing one of them, and it makes my face twist like I'm smelling sour milk. Disgusting. I bet Day would taste like the wintergreen gum he likes to chew.

It's weird, thinking about him like this, and it makes my cheeks hot even in the winter wind. The boys at the bottom of the hill start walking up. My path is clear. It's time.

I hope Dayton sees this.

I take three running steps forward and jump onto the saucer.

It's a mistake.

I know it right away.

I've started too high on the top of the hill. It's way too steep and I can feel the saucer going out of control beneath me but I can't stop with my legs pinned underneath me. All I can do is hold onto the edge and try not to scream. Am I screaming?

Adrenaline rushes through my veins, bright and sharp—*this is what breaking the rules feels like*—and I see everything so clearly, the sunlight dazzling on the puffs of snow rising on the hill, the boulder at the bottom, and the gray saucer spinning in front of me, dropped or thrown by one of those idiot boys.

I tip right to avoid the saucer, picking up speed, but it's another mistake because now I'm barreling toward the boulder and *that will not be good, oh my god that will not be good.*

I overcorrect to the left and almost lose it but then I'm going up, up, over a hill in the snow hidden in all the blinding white and for a few loud beats of my heart I'm airborne, tipping backward *too far backward* and I can see the snow beneath me where I should be seeing sky and then that brilliant snow is speeding toward me.

I try to tuck my head in but it slams into the snow first, my hat tugging off, and suddenly the snow seems more like ice. The saucer comes down next, one edge clipping my lip, and I roll out onto my back, one wet mitten against my mouth, ears ringing.

What did I do?

All those people watching—

My lip throbs, the back of my head throbs, and tears prick the corners of my eyes, which is why it's blurry when a face appears above me, brown eyes wide and worried. It's not Wes. It's Dayton, and with the sun behind his head like this he looks like the handsomest angel ever to have walked the earth.

His lips move but I can't hear him over the ringing in my ears.

"What?" I say, and my voice sounds too loud inside my head.

He crouches next to me and his voice cuts in. "—can you feel your toes? Jesus, you hit the ground *hard*. Summer? You okay? Your arms are probably fine, since you've got that one up." He puts one hand on mine and tugs my mitten away from my lip, then makes a face. "What happened to your lip?"

"The sled." It's puffy against my teeth now. I can see Wes—he's behind Dayton. He must have gotten there second.

"Can you feel your toes?"

I guess I can. I wiggle both feet, but I'm still lightheaded.

"Deep breaths," says Dayton casually, like he's in charge of this situation and every other one too. I take a deep breath and the ringing subsides a little bit. "Damn, you're *tough*." He cracks a smile, shaking his head. "You almost did a total backflip in the air with that thing. I didn't think you'd go for it, but—"

"I didn't. I hit the hill by accident." I try to shove up on one elbow but it makes me dizzy.

Dayton moves fast. "Whoa. Let me help you. That was a hell of a fall." He puts one hand on my arm and the other around my back and everywhere he touches me my skin glows. I take as long as I can standing up, then one last deep breath. Day stands close. He's tall. Taller than I remembered him being. I want him to stand this close for the rest of the day. I want everyone to see him standing with me.

But the only person who seems to notice is Wes, who's watching Dayton with narrowed eyes, sled dangling from his hand. "You okay?" He says finally.

"Yeah." No thanks to him. I used to think he was a hero, but he doesn't look like one standing next to Day.

"Good." He rubs a hand against his forehead, under his hat, then turns his attention to Dayton. "You want to get some pizza?"

4

SHE THINKS I'M A HERO.

That's problem number one. Her eyes lit up at the sight of me. Her cheeks went a delicate pink. And she ran across the room to hug me like I never broke her heart. In Summer Sullivan's eyes, I'm still a good man.

Problem number two?

Her shirt is distracting.

It's a dress shirt, a dark blue that brings out the vivid hue of her eyes, and it's completely appropriate for an office setting. But it's *fitted,* and when she turns to her computer to pull up my file, I stifle the urge to leap across the desk and run my hands over the curves the fabric is hiding. It has five buttons and a ruffled bit at the bottom that did more than accentuate her ass while she walked in front of me. I might not have a left foot, but I could undo all of them before she could gasp.

Don't get me started about that ass.

"Is it okay if I call you Dayton?" The question wrenches me away from a juvenile fantasy involving her breasts and my face—Jesus, where did *that* come from?—and it takes too much time for it to compute.

"What else would you call me?"

"Mr. Nash." Her cheeks go pink. She can't hide it. I want to run my thumb over her cheekbone and my fist tightens in my lap.

"We're not strangers." I say it like I don't care.

An emotion flickers across her face, too subtle for me to capture and name. "Not total strangers, anyway." I'd give anything to know what she's thinking right now. She scrolls a few more times, her elegant fingers quick on the mouse, and turns to face me. "Let's start with a little bit about how we can help you."

How we can help you makes my stomach curdle. I don't want help. I especially don't want Summer's help. But her face is wide open, and as much as I want to get the hell out of here, I can't force myself to leave. I settle for a nod.

Summer takes a quick breath in. "Great." She's relieved. We're on solid ground, at least for the moment. "Heroes on the Homefront is primarily a job placement service, but we also offer assistance with arranging medical care, finding suitable living arrangements, and connecting you with fellow veterans who may be—"

I thought I could let this speech roll over me, but *fellow veterans* is too much.

"No. I don't need any of that."

She bites her lip, eyes lowering to the calendar at the center of her desk, and a wave of regret crashes into me at chest height. I reach out to her folded hands before I know what I'm doing and catch myself at the last minute. I'm not going to hold her fucking hand, but the movement has caught her eye and those blues are on mine again, every bit of me mesmerized by the color.

"I'm—" I clear my throat. "I don't think I need that, but go ahead and finish."

Summer's smile is brilliant like sun on the sand. "There wasn't much more to say. Only that we offer support groups and one-on-one meet-ups between veterans who may be able to connect via common experiences." Her words come out in a tumble, and when she's finished speaking she blows a breath out through her lips and reaches up to tuck a nonexistent flyaway behind her ear. That's what she always did when she was relieved, and seeing it nearly gives me a heart attack. Maybe she's not so different.

"All right. I don't think I'll need those things, but if I do—"

"If you do, here's my card." She leans forward and takes a card from a holder at the edge of the desk, sliding it across the surface toward me with a grin. *Summer Sullivan,* right there in big letters. *Career Placement Coordinator* underneath. "Those came in yesterday," she says, pride on display.

I look into her eyes and do my best to keep my head above water. "Yesterday? How long have you been here?"

"Three months." Summer leans back, keeping her head high. "I graduated in December and got hired straight out of college."

College. That's what she was doing while I was in the desert, and then doing even less savory things back in the states. My throat tightens at the life not lived. If I'd done that—if I'd done a *lot* of things differently—

I can't go down that road right now. Summer has shaken off her burst of pride and switched back into professional mode. "So, career placement." Her eyes track over my arms, barely fitting into the dress shirt from lifting so many windows and frames. "What kinds of jobs are you interested in?"

"I'm supposed to ask about clerical work." I can't help sounding bitter.

She takes it in stride. "All right. Something without a lot of heavy lifting, then. Let me take another look at your resume and I can see—"

My right hand curls into a fist on top of my knee as she scans the screen again. "I'm seeing Army experience here, honorable discharge, then nine months with Killion Glass, most recently a..." Her voice fades out as she reads. "Level 2 Processor? Did that give you any management experience?"

I didn't expect this conversation to happen with Summer. "No. Level 2 means I stand at the end of the row for most of the day and lift finished windows into racks for delivery." It sounds fucking pathetic, and up until now, I didn't care.

"You're still at Killion?"

"Until I can find replacement work."

"Mm-hmm." Her mouth twists in an unconscious pout. "The main issue I see is this gap of almost—" She does quick math. "Looks like ten months. Were you recovering?"

Summer doesn't say from what. "Or volunteer work? If it was volunteer work, we can add a section to the resume, which will look pretty attractive to—"

I don't want to think about it. For fuck's sake, I wish she'd leave it alone.

"It wasn't volunteer work." Her eyes fly back to my face, but she doesn't look surprised at the tone. She hides it well.

"All right," she says softly, then tries again. "If there's anything you'd like to share, I can help with phrasing so it's not so glaring."

My throat is thick with rage at what I did. For being so *stupid*. But there's no way I can explain that to her. If I get through this without flying off the handle, it'll be a small miracle. "It wasn't volunteer work." The words are almost a growl. I can feel the howling blackness surging up from my gut. I'm supposed to be past this. I'm supposed to be *long past this.*

"Day," Summer says, looking me straight in the eye, a little half smile on her face. Does she know she's calling me back from the brink? How could she? "It's all right. Let's move on."

5

Ten Years Ago

BENTLEY DAVIS IS the biggest asshole on the *planet*.

I feel so stupid I could die. I could die, right here in the high school gym. My chest is tight and achy underneath the gorgeous pale pink dress my mom and I spent two hours picking out at the mall. Nobody's noticed the dress. They're all busy laughing at me.

Tears threaten at the corners of my eyes. It's a gross hot shame and I hate it. I swallow the lump in my throat and retreat farther back into the corner, watching the multicolored lights from the DJ's stand soar over the gym.

"Your dress is killer," someone says off my elbow. It does nothing to dull the pain.

"Thanks." It's a dull, quiet response, meant to push them away, but he laughs.

"Sunny, what's got you down?" His voice is warm and

familiar and sexy and *oh my god* it's Dayton, over here in this abandoned corner with me.

"What are you doing here?" I blurt it out like an idiot, but he and Wes weren't coming to the dance.

He laughs again. "That's some greeting for your favorite person on the planet."

It makes me laugh too, a silvery happiness unfolding at the center of my rib cage. "Who said you were my favorite person on the planet?"

Day gives me a knowing look. "Don't say it out loud, Sunny. I know." He sounds like he's joking. Is he joking?

I steal a glance at the rest of Dayton and wish I could have a picture of how he looks right now. Dark jeans, tight enough to hug the muscles of his legs, and a white collared shirt, the sleeves pushed up to his elbows. The lights keep landing in his dark hair and flickering away. He looks hot. Hot enough to have a date, which reminds me of my own horribly embarrassing situation. He sees my face fall into a frown. I hope he doesn't see the surge of tears.

"Hey," he says. "Are you okay?"

I cross my arms over my chest, clutch in one hand. "Yes. I'm fine."

He nudges me with an elbow and I'm breathless at the touch. "Tell me the truth."

If I tell him the truth, I might cry in front of him, and I don't want to do that. It's bad enough that everyone in school has seen me standing here. They don't also need to witness me having a breakdown over a stupid joke, even if I'm the punchline.

But there he is, waiting me out.

I take a shuddering breath. "My date stood me up." I say it as the music gets loud, a throbbing beat, hurting my ears.

"What?"

"My date stood me up," I shout just as the song ends and the sound cuts out for one godforsaken instant. Yes. I *am* going to die here.

Dayton doesn't hesitate. The DJ is scrambling for another song and in the last gap before the next one Dayton yells, "My date stood me up too!" A few people at the edge of the crowd laugh. One girl grabs her friend's elbow and points at me. For once, I'm not standing here by myself. I'm standing with Dayton Nash, and the sheer pleasure of it makes me weak in the knees.

The next song starts and I find the courage to step a little closer. "Did your date really stand you up?"

"Nah," Dayton says, eyes scanning the crowd. "I didn't have a date. Wes decided he wanted to come at the last minute."

Even I know what that's about. "Corinne?"

"Corinne," he confirms, shooting me a sidelong look. "You think she's his type?"

I don't know what to say. Wes scored big when he got Corinne Fletcher to date him. She's popular. She's a *cheerleader*. But to me, she seems cold. Maybe opposites *do* attract. Although Wes isn't always *nice*.

"I don't know," I say with a sigh. "I don't know what my own type is. It's definitely not Bentley Davis."

"That prick stood you up?"

"He invited me here." The lump rises in my throat again. "But he didn't show up."

"And then those goons of his probably laughed behind their hands like a bunch of limp-dick assholes."

"Dayton!" I dissolve into laughter and he follows me. "I can't believe you said that."

"Listen, Sunny—" I wish he'd stop calling me that. That's what my *family* calls me, and I don't want him to be my family. I want him to be...something else entirely. I also don't want him to stop talking. "Bentley Davis is a piece of shit with a stupid name." I snort out loud. He *does* have a stupid name. "He's an ass and he doesn't deserve you. Look at you. You're gorgeous."

It might not be so bad to die of happiness. "I—thanks, Day."

"I mean it." He looks me in the eye. "You look beautiful tonight, and it's Bentley's loss. But you know what?"

"What?" I can't look away from him. I don't ever want to look away from him. He's so tall and handsome and *good*.

"Boys grow up." He gestures vaguely at the dance floor. "One day, they'll be ready for you. Wait for a man, Sunny."

My heart stops, sings. *Wait for a man.* The way he's looking at me, how close he's standing—could he mean...does he mean...wait for *him*?

"Nash!" Someone screams his name from the middle of the dance floor and he turns with a smile.

"What?" He shouts back.

They say something unintelligible but he must understand it, because the moment between us breaks into pieces. "Okay," he answers at the top of his lungs, then turns back to me one more time. "It'll be all right, Sunny. Go dance. Have some fun. You've got time." He brushes his fingertips against my bare shoulder, sending goosebumps running down the length of my arm, and then he jogs away, into the center of the crowd.

I have a big, ridiculous grin on my face and I can't catch my breath. I don't dare think the word *love*. But thinking of Dayton saying *limp-dick assholes* makes me laugh again. When the arm comes down around my shoulders, I'm certain it's him and get ready to look up into his face. He probably came back to make *sure* I'm fine. Day would do that. I look up mid-laugh, and the sound dies in my throat.

"God, Wes, what are you doing?"

He's hot and vaguely sweaty. I imagine he and Corinne have been going at it in that crowd of people for as long as he's been here. Or maybe they've been doing something else. Gross.

"How's my little sister?"

"Fine without you." I try to disengage from his arm but he holds on tight. "Let me go, Wes."

"I wanted to chat with you."

"You never want to *chat* with me. Go dance with your girlfriend."

"She's in the bathroom. Don't fall in love with him, Sunny."

"What?"

"Day." He nods toward Dayton, who's in and out of view behind all the other people. "He's not...right for you."

"I'm not in love with him."

"Keep it that way, okay?"

"Fine." I shove him off me again. "Why are you telling me this? Don't you have anything better to do?"

Wes sticks his hands in his pockets, not looking at me. "I saw you guys talking. I know he's good-looking." Now he does meet my eyes. "But there's something about him that scares me."

"Who *are* you?" I've never known my brother to be scared of anything. Ever. "He's your best friend. Stop being weird."

"He is my best friend," he admits. "I love the guy. But there's more than meets the eye. It's a brotherly warning."

For a lot of years, I've wanted Wes to pay attention to me. Not like this, though. "Thanks."

Corinne comes up behind him and snakes her arms around his shoulders. She whispers something in his ear and his face lights up. "See you later, Sunny." She pulls him away. "Go dance!" He yells over his shoulder.

"Ew, Summer, get away from your brother!" Oh, thank god. My best friend has *arrived,* and even though she's wearing leather pants and a halter top, she looks *incredible.* "I'm here. Let's dance."

"But you weren't—I didn't—"

"Let's *dance.*" She grabs my hand and drags me out to the dance floor, and that's where we stay for the next ninety minutes.

Amy is a good dancer, and I get swept up in her enthusiasm. She finds us a group to dance with and *commits,* and even as people start leaving, she never wavers.

Then, out of nowhere, Dayton is with her.

She beckons him with one finger and laughs out loud, and because Day is who he is, he plays along, pretending to be reeled in. He has no reason to be in this group—he's too old, too *cool*—but he dances like he doesn't care, his body lithe beneath the jeans and shirts.

I must be beet-red, dancing this close to him, but I'm not going to let it show. No way.

This close to the speakers the music overwhelms everything, so I don't hear him speak. I only see him reach out for my hand, a welcoming smile on his face, and in light of everything I take it. What could be so bad about dancing with him? There are tons of people around. Everyone's having fun.

Dayton twirls me into his chest and spins me back out, and just like that, I can dance. He laughs, eyes dancing, and twirls me again. This time, when I'm close, I catch the words *most beautiful* and a warm, rumbling laughs. A slow dance starts and Day sings along, something about *before I met you* and he tosses my arms around his neck like they belong there. We sway together for a few beats and then he dances away, hamming it up. I've never seen him act this ridiculous but I don't mind it. It's making me feel less like crap.

It's making me high on giggles. I can't help it.

A hand closes over my wrist, too tight, too strong, and I stop dead. Or at least I try to stop dead. It doesn't work because Wes is wrenching me to the edge of the crowd, his eyes black with fury. "Did you hear what I said?" he shouts over the music. "*Stay away from him.*"

Rage like heat lightning crackles over me and I twist my arm from his grasp. "Don't *touch* me," I hiss, hoping he catches every word. "Leave me alone, Wes."

He tries to block my way back to the dancers. "He's dangerous."

"He's Dayton. *Leave me alone.*" I shove him, hard, and go past.

"Fine," Wes shouts after me. "It's your funeral." I turn my head as he spins away, back to Corinne. What's *wrong* with him? Dayton is his best friend. Why is he being like this?

"Fuck you," I whisper under my breath. He doesn't hear me. I didn't have the courage to say it to his face. Not something so wrong. It still feels good to say it.

There are fifteen minutes left of the dance, and I'm not going to waste a second talking to my asshole of a brother.

I'm back in the group, next to Amy, across from Dayton, when it occurs to me. Maybe I'll never talk to Wes again. How about that?

6

DAYTON

THE SUMMER I used to know would've retreated into a hidden corner for a while to smooth over the awkwardness of being in the same room with me.

Not this Summer.

She might have flinched when I interrupted her, but she's not a delicate flower and it strikes me that she does this *all day.* The Sunny who would go past her brother's room like a shadow while we played stupid video games is utterly calm, moving briskly on to the next part of our chat, which mainly focuses on my interests.

I don't tell her what my interests were before I got the job at Killion. Those are not the kinds of things that get you a job.

"This is going to sound stupid," I say finally.

One corner of her mouth raises in a smile, but it's not mocking or condescending. "I want to know."

Something twists at the center of my chest. Maybe I should get up and walk away before I tell her everything—all the things she doesn't need to know. Instead, I tap my fist against my rib cage and clear my throat. "I'm interested in problem-solving. Analysis. That kind of thing." In the Army, I'd finally been promoted to a position where I was allowed to attend some low-level mission coordination meetings. If it weren't for my foot getting blown off, I might be doing that kind of thing now.

"That's good," Summer says, her gaze far away. "That's good to know." Then she smiles at me, back in my part of the universe, and stands up. "Let me show you the rest of the office."

I stand up to follow her. "Are we done?"

"I think we've gone over all I need to get started on leads." Her voice is so even, so *soothing,* that I almost believe she can find me a job that isn't total shit. It doesn't sit right, because she's not supposed to be the one bailing *me* out, but I follow her out into the hallway.

"Hazel is my next-door office neighbor," she says easily as we pass the first doorway, and a woman with copper hair gives a wave without missing a beat in her phone call. "She's great at finding places for veterans to take advantage of the GI Bill, and I don't know, maybe your feelings about college have changed."

Summer gives me a mischievous grin and laughs, and they rush back to me—the afternoons Wes and I spent shitting on all the guys from our grade who were going to *take the easy way out at some cushy university and graduate to soft lives.* We had a better plan. We were going to be heroes first.

Look how that turned out.

Even so, being reminded of my unimpeachably cool teenage years makes me laugh, too. "I've grown out of that opinion."

"That's great!" she says brightly. "There are lots of options in the city. I'll be sure to look for placements that will leave you time to attend classes."

A laugh tumbles out of me. "How long can you keep this up?"

"What?" Summer pauses outside another office.

"Look at me. You can see me sitting in a classroom with all those little—" I stop myself short. "College isn't in the cards."

"Oh, stop." She reaches out and slaps me lightly on the shoulder. It takes my breath away. It's been years since anyone had the balls to do that.

We're back at the front door and Summer hands me my coat. When did I take it off? When did she take it? It all happened so...naturally.

"Can you be here tomorrow at eleven? I'll have a list a mile long of people who can't *wait* to hire you." Her eyes are flecked through with the spring light like sun rays on Harbor Lake.

"Yeah." I'm supposed to have a shift at Killion, but I'll reschedule. If the bosses don't like it, then to hell with them. "I'll be here."

Summer smiles up at me and shakes her head a little. "I had no idea it was going to be you."

I wish it wasn't me. I wish this was any other circumstance. "Surprise."

She wrinkles her nose, grinning. "You're exactly the same."

Before I can protest, she slips her arms around my waist again, pulling me in tight, with a sigh that breaks me. And because Summer Sullivan is in the business of twisting the knife, she rises up on tiptoes and presses a gentle kiss against my cheek. "See you tomorrow, Day."

Then I'm outside in the cold, and when I turn around she's joking with the receptionist. I hold myself back from crashing straight through the glass. I want to be in there, with her, not out here, with reality.

In my boot, my missing left foot cramps, clear and strong, the pain shooting up to my knee.

I GAVE SUMMER A FAKE ADDRESS.

I think about it on the train, on the way back to Queens. If she sends me anything in the mail, it'll never arrive. Better to take that risk than have her know where I'm staying.

It's a fucking dive.

By the time I get to the decaying third-floor walk-up, my residual limb feels like it's on fire. It's sliding around in the ill-fitting socket, the gel lining worn through in places. There'll be raw skin under there. Hot spots. I'm fumbling for the key, gritting my teeth against the pain, when my room-mate opens the door.

He's drunk. High. Both. Music spills out from behind his back into the hallway, loud and screaming, and a waiflike girl goes past wearing nothing but the remains of a black bra. There are more of them inside. I don't have to see them to know.

"Naaaaash," drawls Curtis, who's holding a fifth of vodka in one hand, dangling it from his fingers like a purse he's forgotten about. "Where have you been?"

"A meeting." I push past him into the apartment. Last time I saw Curtis, he was getting out of the Army. One three-year contract and he was done. Not cut out for it. He's not cut out for hard drugs, either, but that hasn't stopped him. In the middle of the living room floor, one of Curtis's friends is coiled around the girl with the bra. There's a small silver tray on the carpet next to them. "Jesus. It's two in the afternoon."

I have to get the fuck out of here.

Curtis's eyes are sunken into his skull. Turns my stomach. "It's never too early to party, man. Do a couple lines. Relax."

"I'm good." I'm clawing my way *out* of this hellhole. There's no time to relax.

It's a piercing pain to sidestep him and when I do he bows to me with a languid laugh. I have to get to my room. I keep it locked when I'm out. Sweat beads on my forehead while I force the key into the lock, push the door open, and drag myself inside.

I have a rickety desk chair, the only furniture aside from my bed, and I sink into it with a sharp exhale and pull my leg out of the prosthesis as gently as I can.

I'm going to need some antiseptic.

Worse, I forgot to shut the door.

Curtis sidles in and leans against the frame. "Nash, buddy."

"I'm not going out again. You've had enough."

"I came to deliver a *message*. Don't shoot." He raises his hands in the air, spilling vodka on the carpet outside my door.

"What message?"

"I heard something at the bodega today."

I push myself up from the chair and hop toward the bathroom door. It's the smallest bathroom on the face of the planet, but the only—*only*—silver lining of this place is that I have it to myself. "Spit it out."

"Alexei is looking for you."

I stop dead at the bathroom door, sweat turned to ice at my temples. "What did you say?"

He repeats it again.

"Fuck."

I don't realize I've said it out loud until Curtis responds. "Don't worry, bro." He takes a swig out of the bottle and grins at me, teeth sharp in the dim light of my bedroom. "I didn't say a *thing*. He doesn't know how to find you." He crosses two fingers and presses them over his heart even as he sways back into the hallway. "I'll never tell him you're here."

7

SUMMER

My APARTMENT DOOR flies open in front of me, my keys chiming against the door.

"Oh my god—"

Whitney, my roommate, strikes a pose, head tilted back, arms locked out in the door frame. "Are. You. Ready."

"Whit—"

"For the weeeeeeeeekeeeeennnnnnd!" She stretches the word out like an announcer at a rowdy sporting event, framing it with bright red lipstick, then points at me. "Are you?"

"It's Thursday." I adjust my tote bag on my shoulder. It's impossible not to smile at her. "You know this."

"Touché. But at the stroke of midnight, the weekend is here."

"No, *Friday* is here. Are you going to let me in?"

Whitney gives me an exaggerated pout and slinks away from

the door. She's wearing her favorite black pants. They're her favorite because, as she says, *they go from day to night with a swish of the hips.* "You're no fun."

I swim up out of the daydream I've been tending since the moment Dayton walked out of my office. In the daydream, when he disappears from view, I chase after him. Beg for a few minutes of his time. We end up in a cozy Italian restaurant two blocks down. Somehow a hotel becomes involved. If Whitney hadn't thrown open the door, I might have gotten all the way to the room, to the bed, to the hot pink vibrator she got me as a joke for my birthday senior year. I found out later it's a high-quality piece. *Definitely* not a joke.

I drop my keys on the little table in the entryway and unwind my scarf from my neck. "I'm extremely fun. When it's appropriate."

Whitney turns around, shaking her head. "Fun is always appropriate. We only have—"

"—one life to live," I finish for her. Coat on hook. Scarf on hook. Purse on hook. Everything in its place. "I know."

"And yet you look like you're headed for a pair of flannel pajamas and a book."

She's so right that it's a little offensive. I smile rapturously. "What could be better on a Thursday night?"

Whitney's eyes light up. "Drinks."

"No."

"Drinks at Vino Veritas."

I cross my arms over my chest. "That's not fair, and you know it."

Whitney folds her hands in front of her. "Come on, Sunny, it's an exciting day!"

"Why? Did something happen at work?"

Her smile is worth a gigawatt at least. "*Technically,* it was at work."

I gasp. "Did you get an audition?"

"Not just an audition." Whitney does spirit fingers. "A *second* audition. I got a callback!"

Then it's all jumping and shrieking in the entryway, right up until Whit hustles me into my coat and scarf and down to our favorite wine bar.

"WE HAVE *CELEBRATED*," I tell her ninety minutes later. We're tucked into a table by the front window and neither of us cares about the view onto 9th Avenue. "Let's get the bill."

"Not a *chance*," says Whitney, motioning for the waiter. "One last drink. Two glasses of your sweetest moscato," she says to him extravagantly. We've already shared a bottle and some of the prettiest appetizers you'll find in the city. I'm pleasantly buzzed but there it is in the back of my mind—the call of work. Getting up early. Getting to bed at a decent hour. It's the right thing to do. I have to be at my best for the veterans.

It's all true. It's also true that the wine has made my heart feel steady for the first time since Dayton looked at me across that waiting room.

"Tell me your news. There has to be news." Whitney leans

across the table, eyes shining, her voice bright over the rumble and roll of the conversation in the bar.

"Just another day in the office."

"Liar. Your face is beet red."

"I've had half a bottle of wine."

"*Sunny.*"

That delirious joy shot through with dread blooms in my chest. "I shouldn't say anything. All of my meetings are confidential." My voice wobbles a bit on *confidential* and Whitney pounces.

"What happened?" She grabs my hand on the surface of the table. "Tell me right now."

I bite my lip. I shouldn't say anything. I'm not supposed to disclose anything about the veterans to anyone else, and I'm sure this is outside the rules. But I'm humming with the sight of him. If I don't release some of this pressure, how am I going to sleep tonight? The scale tips in Whitney's favor. Damn it.

"I ran into...an old friend." It's ridiculously inadequate, calling him that, but that's the only way around this. I'm not breaking the rules if I'm only mentioning that I saw a childhood buddy.

Whitney gasps. "Who?"

He's dangerous. My brother's words from a million years ago rocket through my mind. His voice rising at home the next day. The freeze that's grown between us ever since. "Dayton."

Whit rolls her eyes and drops my hands. "That's a city in Ohio. Are you that drunk?"

"Dayton Nash." I say it louder and her eyes go wide. Something clicks in her mind, her eyebrows shooting up toward her hairline. "My brother's—"

"—best friend," she says, and covers her mouth with her hand. "Oh, my god."

"Ex best friend," I say automatically, because that's what it is now, isn't it?

She tilts her head down, looking up at me from beneath her lashes. "You always had a crush on him, didn't you? I bet he was *hot*. I bet he's still hot. I bet your heart went *boom* when he walked through the door." Whit's mouth drops open. "Did you *sleep with him*?"

"Oh, my *god*."

"You did, didn't you?"

"*No*," I shriek. "I did not sleep with him in my office!"

"Two glasses of moscato," says the waiter from five inches away. He can't disguise the laughter in his voice.

Perfect.

8

SUMMER

Eight Years Ago

MY MOTHER CLUTCHES my arm right above the elbow as the boys—*men*—march out onto the field in the Georgia heat. We spent half the night and most of the morning taking two different planes to get here, and for an instant I think she's cracking up.

She claps her other hand over her mouth. "Oh, Sunny, look at him."

They all look the same—they're supposed to, in those uniforms. I can't see him.

Then I can.

Dayton is one of the first soldiers out on the parade field, marching side by side with all the others he and Wes went to boot camp with. I've never thought that much about men in the service but watching Day's body move beneath the camouflage fabric of his uniform, my breath catches. I didn't think it was possible for him to look stronger, but his face is leaner somehow, *harder.* It's Dayton, but different. I can see it from where we're sitting, the humid Georgia air soaking into our skin.

"Oh, he's *changed,*" Mom breathes, leaning closer.

"Yeah, he has."

The company turns a sharp left, coming around the corner of the parade field and *pop,* there's Wes. He's the one my mom's been looking at. He's the one I didn't notice because he was shoulder to shoulder with Dayton.

"Mrs. Sullivan, it's not a big deal."

"Dayton." My mom puts on her best stern-mother expression and grabs him right above his elbow. "We can't celebrate without you."

His eyes move from her face to the crowd around us. The wide sidewalk outside the National Infantry Museum is mobbed with families, each orbiting around a boot camp graduate in green. Day's family must be late. Things happen with planes all the time. Our flight out of Atlanta was almost delayed when the crew went over on their shift time.

"It's all right, Mrs. Sullivan."

"Come on, man. It's dinner at Applebees." Wes cajoles him from where he stands next to me. "Don't put up a fight." I don't like the edge in my brother's voice but Day gives a little shake of his head.

"If you've got room."

"The rental's a zippy SUV with third-row seating," my mom tells him, beaming. "Plenty of room."

Day gives the crowd one more glance.

Then he gives in, and we all ride to Applebees in the rental car.

"THEY SAY we could deploy as early as six months out." Wes stabs a knife into his steak and takes a bite, back straight, his pride puffing him out. He was in good shape before he left for boot camp. He's in better shape now. I keep my eyes on my burger. Wes looks good, but he's my *brother*.

Dayton looks so good I can't look at him without blushing.

Dad chuckles, but I see him swallow hard. "You're in a bit of a rush, don't you think?"

Wes shakes his head slowly. "I want to get on with it. Six weeks of AIT and I'll be good to go." He rubs his hands together.

"What's AIT?" I ask the question with a sidelong glance at Wes. Things haven't been the same between us since that dance, but I want to know how much longer he's going to be in training. How much longer *Day* is going to be in training.

"Advanced Individual Training." Day's the one who answers. Unlike Wes, who's sawing at his steak like he's been starving, Day has been methodically making his way through a chicken sandwich and mashed potatoes. "More specific training for the jobs we'll be doing once we get our post assignments." His voice is hypnotizing. I'm staring. I can't help it. In the world's smoothest move, I grab a fry from my plate and shove it into my mouth.

"Cool."

"It *is* cool, sis." His voice carries over to the next table. "But it'll be even cooler when we deploy. When we're *really* getting stuff done." His eyes glow at the thought of it. Who *is* this guy? When we were kids, Wes *lost it* over a cat we had that got run over by a car. Now he's all about heading off to war and *getting stuff done*. I don't feel like eating any more of my burger.

"What about you, Dayton? Do you have plans for after you're done with AIT?" Mom's voice is mild.

The corner of Dayton's mouth turns upward. "It won't be up to me, Mrs. Sullivan. I'll get my post and deploy, probably about the same time as Wes."

"And after?" My mom sets her jaw. "After you both get back from deployment, what will you do? Is this a career for you, too?"

Dayton puts down his fork. "I'm not sure."

"Hell of a thing to be unsure about, son." Dad reaches for his beer and surveys Dayton across the table.

Day meets his gaze, head on. "It's a chance for me to get away."

For the first time all afternoon, the smile disappears from Wes's face. What's that about? I've heard the rumors about Day and what he supposedly did, but why would *Wes* feel guilty about it.

"You'll send us your updated address as soon as you have it?

Both of you." My mom signals for the waiter. "I've been out of water for ten minutes and I'm parched. Anybody else?"

"I'LL CATCH a bus back to the post."

"Dayton—"

"Give you some time to spend together before your flight out," Dayton says, flashing my mom a confident smile. She can't resist it. This graduation trip has been weeks in the making.

Hugs all around, with a handshake for my dad and Wes. When Day wraps his arms around me I take a deep breath in. He smells of soap and spice and *man* and I keep my face absolutely blank while my insides warm and glow.

Then he's walking across the parking lot toward a bus stop on the outer edge of the property. My mom's phone rings in her purse. Her face lights up when she sees the name on the screen.

"It's your grandfather!" She hands the phone joyously to Wes, and I stifle a sigh. Grandpa is eighty-seven, and *all* he wants to talk about is the honor and privilege of joining the military. And of *course* it's honorable, but it also means that we can't get into the car, because the traffic noise interferes with his hearing aids somehow.

Day stands tall next to the bus stop shelter, his posture perfect. It strikes me to the core. I have to know. I *have* to know what he's running from. What makes him want to get away so badly?

I don't want him to leave. This might be my last chance to tell him so.

"I'll be right back," I say into my mother's ear, and she brushes me off, straining to hear what my grandfather is saying to Wes, and in fifteen seconds I'm up next to Day, heartbeat loud in my ears.

"I didn't believe them." It's not very suave, but they're the first words that come to mind.

He turns, his eyebrows raised in surprise. "Sunny, what are you—"

"I didn't believe the rumors. About that store. I know you didn't do it."

Day's face darkens. "You don't know—"

"I know *you*." It's the truest thing I've ever said. I do know Day. I've known him for years. He's been my brother's best friend for *years,* and I know he wouldn't do what they said he'd done. "You don't have to run away, Dayton, you really don't. I believe in you. I know you're not like that. You can do anything." My breath is fast and fluttery. I can't *believe* I'm saying these things to him. I can't believe I'm standing in his heat like this. Tears prick at the corners of my eyes, like I'm a little kid.

Dayton's eyes never leave mine. His tone softens. "It's not like that, Sunny. I don't have a choice."

"You *do*." I whisper, my voice breaking. I don't know where Wes thinks they're going to go, but I don't want Day to leave. It's too dangerous. It's too awful.

He swallows hard, a sheen over his dark eyes, and a pure

white hope breaks clean over my chest. He's going to stay. He's going to change his mind. I know it.

"I'm going to miss you, Sunny," he says, standing tall, his shoulders broad under the uniform. With one of his big hands on my shoulder, I feel small, childish. "Be safe, okay?"

My heart shatters.

"Day—"

One step. That's all it takes for him to reach me, to fold me in his arms, and *kiss me.*

My gasp disappears between his lips, and then it's all heat and light and spice, and this is the best moment I've ever lived.

"Hey, asshole!"

Moment over.

9

"WE'VE MADE AN *AMAZING* START." Summer beams at me from the other side of her desk, printouts fanned in front of her. *We.* As if I've done anything other than show up. "I've got six firms with open positions, so I thought we could work through the application process together."

"Firms?"

"Yes. Firms. Companies." She cocks her head to the side, looks at me over the papers. "You said you were interested in analytics and planning, right?"

"Yeah, but—"

"That's where I started." Summer flips the first paper over so it's facing my direction and rises partway out of her seat. "Gordon & Preyde has an opening in its administrative department. You'd probably start with a lot of mail filing, but I thought, given the circumstances—"

"Gordon & Preyde? Is that a law firm?" Summer nods and I laugh out loud. "I can't work at a law firm."

"Yes, you can."

"No, I *really* can't."

Her blue eyes search mine. "If this is about those rumors from back in high school—"

The memory of it swims up from the depths of my mind. Anxiety prickles at my core but I cover it with a smile. I didn't hold up a grocery store back in high school. It was Wes who wanted a thrill, who walked out with two Zippo lighters in his pockets. I was the one the police went after.

But high school's not the problem with working at a law firm. It's what I did after I got out of the Army.

I'm not going to tell Summer that.

"It's not about that." She keeps it professional, but I see the twitch at the corner of her mouth. I know there's more she wants to say. "What else do you have?"

"A similar position is open at Delaware Paper Products."

"Oh, Jesus. Like that TV show?"

Summer grins. "No. Not like that." She glances over at her computer screen. "It's a start-up that claims to *revolutionize the distribution of paper products across the northeast region.*"

"Sounds like my kind of place." It doesn't. The thought of sweating through dress shirts in an office cubicle while I try to ignore phantom pains does *not* appeal to me, but here we are.

"How about this?" Summer gathers up the papers with a flick of her wrists and pushes the stack toward me. "Why don't you take a look through these, and then we can talk about whichever opportunity—" Her elbow knocks against a mug at the edge of her desk and pens spill onto the carpet on my side of the desk. "Oh—"

She's out of her seat in a flash, but I'm faster. By the time she's around to my side I have the pens in one hand and the mug in the other, and I'm standing to meet her. Her face is bright pink. "Sorry about that."

Summer takes the mug, her hands brushing against mine, and her cheeks get pinker. I didn't think that was possible. If everything had been different, I'd take her face in my hands right now and—

"Day?"

It's not the professional, chipper voice she's been using since she led me back here and offered me a seat.

"Yeah?"

"The pens?"

I can't stop the short, harsh laugh that's on the edge of my lips, but I *can* tip the pens back into the mug. "I think that's all of them."

Summer looks down into the pens and takes a deep breath, a smile playing at the corners of her mouth. I can't say I mind that she's standing this close. "You saved the day," she says softly, and it's all I can do not to reach for her.

"No. I'm not that kind of guy." It's a joke, meant to be light-hearted, but her smile disappears.

Her blue eyes are huge and clear when she looks into mine, the mug trembling in her hands. "Aren't you?"

"I don't—"

"I always thought you were, when I was—when I was growing up." Her eyebrows draw together. "But then after boot camp—" The air around us is charged, every one of my limbs humming with the tension. This is *not* how I expected this conversation to proceed.

"I went where the Army told me to go."

Sunny—that's who she looks like right now, not the professional Summer Sullivan of Heroes on the Homefront— looks toward her window, then back at me. "You went to Afghanistan and you never said a word to me. I thought—" She swallows hard. "I thought you could have died. All that time, I never heard from you. Not once."

In the emptiness of my hands, I feel it again—the dust. The grit. The fine sand that coated everything, got into every crack and crevice. I was never clean in the desert. Never. It settled in every breath. Summer is *right here*. I could finally tell her that with every one of those filthy, dusty breaths, I thought of her. I ached for her.

For that kiss.

It would have been a mistake, to be with her then. Wes proved that.

I thought of her every second. My heart pounds against my rib cage remembering that distance between us, the sun beating down, broiling me inside the uniforms. A bead of sweat gathers at the center of my back and drips down beneath my shirt. This isn't *there*. She's standing right in front of me, her shampoo in the air. I'm breathing her scent. Now. Here. Still that ache, still that hope.

"I couldn't believe it. Not after—" She smiles like she doesn't mean to. "Do you remember the night before you left?"

"How could I forget?" She opens her mouth to reply and my last defense drops to the ground. "I did *this*."

There's a sound of metal twisting and breaking, and it's the sound of all the rules coming apart in my hands. I wrap my palms around her cheeks and her soft skin against mine is a revelation. *Boom.* For the first time since my boots touched American soil, I am fully here, fully in this moment. I kiss her like I kissed her back then and Sunny might be all grown up but her lips part beneath mine. Her hands are on mine and the rest of her melts, her weight pressing into the kiss. She tastes like peppermint and snow.

Alexei is looking for you.

The thought drills in through the sweet taste of her and I break off the kiss. What am I *doing?* Summer can't be near me. She can't be near *that*. She's so much better. Jesus, she's so much better.

She loses her balance and steps forward, onto my prosthesis, hands going to her face, covering her mouth. "I'm—oh, my god, I'm sorry."

I step backward to try and get some space, but the chair is there, so I only gain a few inches. "It's fine. Couldn't feel it."

Summer laughs and turns away, straightening her shirt. She's trying hard to get her professional face on, but it's not working. She clears her throat. "How'd that happen?" Her voice softens again. "Will you tell me?"

Guilt. Pure and strong and cutting. I can't get out from under it, from the high color in her cheeks, from this office, and then a surge of anger, red-hot. At Wes. At myself. At the Army recruiter, at the Taliban who buried the land mine. Summer sees it in my face and bites her lip. I try to keep my voice measured. "If you wanted to know about that—" She braces. "You should've asked your brother."

10

Two Years Ago

"Dance with us. Summer! Dance with us!"

Theresa's voice snaps me out of the thought I'd lost myself in, courtesy of one too many beers, and back into the basement of the biggest house on fraternity row. I knew what the letters were when one of the brothers waved us in through the gate two hours ago. I don't know them anymore.

"I'm dancing."

"You're not *dancing*," she shrieks, tugging me farther into the crowd. "You're standing there, thinking about your hometown hero."

"I don't have a hometown—"

"Army guys aren't for you." She waggles a finger in my face, spilling beer from her cup onto the floor in the process. "You can't spend all of college mooning over some asshole who's too old for you."

Through the drunken sea of my brain I feel a swell of anger. "He's not an—"

Theresa isn't listening to me. "Chris Leavenworth is *into* you."

"What?"

"The *president of the fraternity.*" She enunciates each syllable, her teeth glowing white in the black lights. A flash of red crosses her skin and makes her look like she might burst into flame. "Look! He's the hottest guy here."

He's leaning against the sound system In a polo shirt, blond hair in a neat cut, teeth even and straight. I know about his teeth because he's grinning at me so aggressively that it's almost a leer. I can see why Theresa thinks he's hot. I can see the polo shirt straining to contain the biceps he's almost certainly spent hours in the gym on. Theresa tugs at my elbow, forcing me to sway with the beat. Beer sloshes in my gut.

"He asked me about you," she says into my ear, her breath hot and heavy with alcohol. "He wants to dance with you."

A strobe light flashes off to the side of the crowd and in the burst of light I see what a pretty picture Chris Leavenworth thinks we'd make. He's tall and blond and I'm....not tall, but I have the kind of blonde hair that makes Theresa frown when she thinks I don't see her in the mirror, like she did when we were getting ready to come to this party. She's the one who thought I should wear the red dress that comes down *one single inch* beneath my ass and four-inch heels.

He wants to dance with you. Chris lifts his chin, sets his drink on the speaker next to him, and steps into the crowd. My heart leaps into my throat. I could do this. I could make out with the president of this frat, I could wrap my body around him on the dance floor and later in his bed, I could let him fuck me, take me, parade me around campus on his arm.

It would be a nice distraction.

I would be *his* distraction, too. Half of my sisters are dying to date Chris Leavenworth, and all of them might get their chance. He's like that. He uses women until they bore him and then he tosses them to the side. Done. Gone.

The floor tilts up toward me and I turn away, leaning toward the edge of the crowd. Theresa's grip tightens on my elbow. "What are you doing? He's coming over here." I shake her off. I need air. I need space. Theresa catches up. "Are you *leaving*? What the hell, Summer?" She's drunk and so am I, and I'm not having this fight with her. Not right now.

"I have to go."

"Because a hot guy is interested in you?" Her face twists into an exaggerated parody of disgust. "Fine. Go home and get yourself off thinking about some soldier who's probably fucking somebody else halfway around the world." My mouth drops open and drunk Theresa wilts in the face of my shock. "Summer," she says, and drops her half-empty Solo cup to the floor so she can press her hands together. "I didn't mean it. Stay at the party. Talk to Chris. He's coming to talk to you. Stay. Please?"

She's begging me to forget about Dayton and I won't do it. I might be drunk and dressed to be seen, to be swept up by Chris Leavenworth, but I won't. I won't. "No," I tell her. My balance is too shaky for heels. As soon as I'm out on the sidewalk, I can get rid of them. "No. I'm going home."

THE SCREAMING SOUND happens again and again and again, close to my ear. Too close. Who's screaming and why is it so loud? I twist away from the sound and my cheek connects with a cool section of pillow. *Please. Please go away and let me sleep.* My head throbs. Turning over in bed is all it's going to take. I never should have gone to that party.

The sound curls in on itself and I reach for whatever, *whoever* is screaming. My hands make contact with my phone, shoved halfway under my pillow.

It's ringing.

The sound resolves into my ringtone.

Shit.

Is it an alarm? Am I missing something? Did I sleep all weekend into Monday?

I scramble for the phone, my stomach lurching. *Way* too much beer. Way too many dreams, the frat house becoming the mountains in Afghanistan, where my brother and Dayton are on their third deployment in six years.

It's my mom.

The ringtone cuts out, showing the alerts on my screen. Twelve missed calls in a row, all of them from my mom's phone.

My fingers are slow on the screen and it rings before I can call her back.

"Hello?" Saying the word makes me want to throw up.

"Summer, I've been trying to call you." Her voice is frantic. "Where have you been?"

"I was—I was asleep, Mom, I'm sorry." My mouth tastes horrible. I don't know what's more urgent—brushing my teeth or throwing up.

"Get up, Summer. I've been trying to call."

I swing my legs over the side of the bed. Another mistake. It's my fault I feel this way. I should have been more responsible last night. "I'm up. What's wrong, Mom?"

"There was an accident."

"An accident?" My mind is still flooded with beer, with sleep. "Who was in an accident? Was it Dad?"

"No. Your brother. He and Dayton were in a Humvee, out on some mission, and—"

I'm going to throw up. My mom lets out a sharp breath. "Is he—"

There's a low murmuring in the background of the call, and then my dad is on the line.

"Summer, this is your father. There's been an accident involving your brother."

My lungs are tight, compressed, and I can hardly draw a breath. This is why I've been forcing myself to talk to Wes when he's on leave. This is the only reason. *In case...* "Is he—"

"He's all right. Cuts and bruises. It was a near thing."

"Oh, my god." The relief is so strong I almost puke from that. Dread comes fast on its heels. "Dad—"

"He's going to be fine, honey. He has enough time to call you, but not much more." He says something about international calls, the Army—I don't hear any of it. "Stay by your phone."

He hangs up.

I stare at the phone in my hands. My bedroom at the sorority house rocks from side to side. I can't run to the bathroom. I can't be back in time for my brother's call. I stay where I am.

The phone rings in my hand, a strange number.

"Hello?"

"Hey, Sunny, it's me."

His voice is rough, a little broken by the connection. "Wes." My throat closes and I swallow, clearing it. "Mom and Dad said—"

"Yep," he says, as if this is no big deal, as if this happens on a daily basis. "We had an encounter with a land mine. My knee got pretty fucked up by the shrapnel, but it'll be all right. I'm in the hospital. Surgery—in three weeks—and back to the—"

"I'm so glad you're okay." Hot tears slip down my cheeks. I can't stand Wes. I can't stand what he did to Dayton after he kissed me. But he could have *died.* Horror builds in my gut, mixing with the beer, and goosebumps spread like wildfire along my shoulders and arms.

"I'll be just fine," Wes says. He sounds like he did when we were kids. He'd protect me from spiders I found in my bedroom, and when nobody else was watching, he was sweet to me. Strong. "There's no need to worry, Sunny."

I gulp in a breath. "I'm really hungover, Wes."

He laughs out loud. "Party hard last night?"

"Yeah. I didn't think—I didn't know—"

"No way you could have known. It's all going to work out anyhow. I'll be out of here in no time and back running missions."

"Wes?"

"Yeah?"

"What about Day? Mom said—" My hands are shaking so badly I can hardly hold onto the phone. "She said Dayton was with you in the Humvee."

He laughs again, all sharp edges and ridicule, and every shred of sweetness is gone. "With me? Yeah, that asshole was with me. If he hadn't been with me, that would have been something. A completed mission, more like."

I am speechless. What do I say? There isn't enough air in the room.

"Wes—" I croak out his name. "You're—you're in the hospital."

"Damn right I am."

"Is Day there? Is he with you?" Every word I say to him digs deeper into the rift between us. I know it and I can't help it. I have to know. "Is he okay?"

There's a silence so long I wonder if he's hung up on me.

"Wes?"

"I have no idea," he says flatly. "If he got hurt, that's his problem not mine." I close my eyes. "I told you to stop asking about him."

11

SUMMER

"—Hazel was her name, wasn't it? She seemed nice."

I force my attention back to the man sitting across the table from me.

It's supposed to be Dayton, sitting there.

It's not him.

Dayton and I had a follow-up today to finalize plans for one of the firms and work through his application.

He didn't show up.

I'm so pissed at him. How dare he? How dare he kiss me like that and then hide from me like this? When he didn't show up for his eleven o'clock, Carla brought me a walk-in, and I took it.

"She's very good at her job," I say briskly. I've got to steer the conversation back to our services and away from how nice everyone is, which has been the bulk of our talk thus far. "So...Logan." His name comes to me at the last possible moment. "I'd love to talk about what we at Heroes on the Homefront can offer you."

He leans toward me, green eyes oddly pale in the light coming from my window. "What about Hazel? I'd like to see more of *her*."

I look across at him.

Wait a beat.

Smile.

Then I grab some informational pamphlets in a holder on the side of my desk. "Here's the plan." He takes the pamphlets. "You look through these and figure out whether any of our supports might be a good fit. Once you've done that, you can call Carla at the front desk and schedule an appointment." *Not with me.*

He has the grace to look sheepish. "Sounds great. That's a great plan."

I stand up, shoving my chair back from the desk, and stick out my hand for him to shake. "We'll be looking forward to your call."

I let him find his own way out.

As soon as I hear Carla calling *goodbye* in the front office, I shrug myself into my coat and wrap my scarf around my neck. It's sunny today but bitter cold, and I'm going to be walking a bit. I can sense it.

At the doorway to my office I turn back. The stack of papers with job openings for Dayton is out in the center of my desk —I trusted him to *be here*, damn it. I fold them in half with a vengeance and stick them in one of the big pockets of my coat. Wallet and phone. I don't need my purse. I won't be gone *that* long.

Carla raises her eyebrows at me from her ergonomic desk chair. "You headed out early?"

"I have a client meeting."

She purses her lips, but her expression turns into a smile. "Which client? The tall, dark, and handsome one?"

"I—"

"You don't have to tell me, sweetheart. I already know."

I roll my eyes at her and go out into the winter.

Maybe this isn't professional. Maybe this is a dumb idea. I don't care. I'm going to find Dayton and talk to him about these jobs if it's the last thing I do. No, we don't *normally* do home follow-up visits with our clients, but this is a special case. He needs this.

I need this.

Why? Because I spent all weekend thinking about him. About how it felt to stand in the same room with him after all these years. About how clean he tasted, exactly the same as that first kiss at Applebees. It's shitty that Friday's kiss *also* ended in silence between us, a cold front building on the horizon, but I'm not in high school anymore. I'm not letting him get away without a real conversation.

I don't.

I dig out the first paper from the stack in my pocket. It's got Dayton's address on it. No phone number. Did he leave it off on purpose? There's an email and a physical address. That's it.

On the corner I step into the doorway of a Duane Reade and put his address into my phone.

Shit. It's going to take almost an hour to get there. I'm going to have to get the subway at 50th, and then—

Wait.

I zoom in on the map on my screen.

What the hell?

Maybe I put in the address wrong.

I double-check with the paper. It's right there in Day's handwriting. *9801 Liberty Ave.* Ozone Park? That's not in Queens. I *know* he said he's living in Queens.

This address is for an IHOP.

He lied to me.

12

SUMMER

INSIDE THE DUANE READE I stalk back and forth in front of the magazine racks, my heart beating fast. A fake address? *A fake address?* Who does Dayton think he is?

I take a calming breath in and let it out to a count of one-two-three-four while I stare at England's favorite royalty in bright, glossy colors. I repeat the process. I don't feel calm, but I have to *act* calm. I'm in a Duane Reade. I can't be the woman freaking out in the Duane Reade because her *client* stood her up.

God, that's why this stings, isn't it? Because I couldn't help myself. I couldn't think of him as *just a client* when he walked into the office, and I can't do it now.

Treating him like any other client would be the right thing to do.

And yet—

I pull out my phone and the paper and tap out a furious email, then delete the whole thing and start over.

Dear Mr. Nash—

Delete.

Dear Day—

Delete.

Hi Dayton,

I'm writing to check in because I had you scheduled for a meeting at eleven this morning. I wanted to make sure you're all right.

Summer Sullivan

I've sent this kind of email a thousand times before. Most people never answer. The rest tell me that they forgot, or they couldn't get out of the house, or they swear they had the date down for next week.

I shove my phone and the paper into my pocket and leave Duane Reade. The wind is at my back on the way to the office, prodding me along, pushing, *pushing.* It's annoying, how insistent it is.

I'm about to cross in front of the windows when my phone buzzes in my pocket.

Incoming emails.

It'll be the regular work back-and-forth, of course—emails from everyone else in the office, triple confirming things we confirmed yesterday, emails from different firms around the city for different clients, emails, emails, emails.

The fifth one down is from him.

My heart skips, stops, rears to a start.

I open the email.

Hi Summer Sullivan,

I couldn't make it. I'm stuck in an appointment at the VA. Catch you next time.

Dayton

I gasp, right there at the magazine racks at Duane Reade.

That asshole.

The VA hospital is five blocks away.

*****

"Do you have an appointment, miss?"

I don't know whether to bristle at *miss* or ignore it, so I go with ignoring it. My pulse is still hammering away in my veins, my heartbeat too loud. I catch a glimpse of myself in the reflective surface behind the reception desk and *whoa*. I look crazy. I *feel* crazy. I followed Dayton to the VA hospital to give him a piece of my mind.

Get it together.

I put a professional smile on for the woman and take out the papers from my pocket. "I'm meeting Dayton Nash. He should be at an appointment right now."

She gives a little half-frown. "What's your connection to Mr. Nash?" A pointed glance at her computer screen nearly does me in. "For confidentiality reasons, I can't simply—"

"Of course, of course." What am I going to say? I'm buying time by the second, and the longer I stand here looking the way I look, the more expensive those moments are getting. "I just need to—" A flash of a white t-shirt, his coat under his arm. "There he is!"

"Miss—"

I brandish the papers like a shield and move past the desk with all the confidence of a former sorority girl turned professional badass. "I'll deliver these and be out of your way. Thank you. Thank you so much."

"Miss, you can't—"

"*Dayton.*"

The line of his back stops and he sticks his head back around the corner and into the hallway, his dark eyes lighting up with shock.

"Sunny? What are you doing—"

The hall is a line of open doors to exam rooms, doctors in a mix of white coats and uniforms coming in and out. One of them stops dead, looking from his clipboard to Dayton to me. "Do you need something, ma'am?"

I liked *miss* better.

"No," I tell him, flashing that same confident smile, and pick up the pace. I'm going full speed when I reach him and hook my arm into his. He's heavy, muscular, but my momentum wheels us both around the corner and down the next hall.

"Do you mind telling me where we're going?"

I don't slow down. "I hope you're heading for a room where we can talk in *private.*" There's no special smile for him. Not now. Not when he *lied* from me, when he stood me up, after all this time, after that *kiss*—

"I'm in room twenty-eight."

I yank him through the door and slip around behind him to slam it shut. Day gets his balance back and stands tall in the center of the room, arms crossed, eyebrows raised.

"How *dare* you?" I planned a more eloquent speech on the walk here, but looking into his eyes, I can't remember a word of it. "How dare you give me a fake address? Me. *Me.* I'm *Summer Sullivan.*" I shout my own name. It's the height of decorum.

"Exactly," he says with a slow shake of his head. "What are you *doing* here?"

"What am *I* doing here? What are you doing calling me *Sunny* and asking me what I'm doing here?"

Dayton raises both his hands. "That was a mistake—"

My mother always said never to point at anyone, but I jab a finger into his chest. "You showed up for *this.*" I motion to the room. It doesn't get more generic doctor's office than this. "You showed up here but not to an appointment with me?"

Day lets out a sharp breath. "Some things are more important than others, I guess."

"I hope you're being sarcastic."

"What could I possibly have to be sarcastic about? You followed me here, into a *doctor's appointment,* and—"

"Yeah. Yeah, I did." My voice is rising and I can't stop it. "I did follow you here. I wanted to know why you *lied* to me about where you were living. Unless you live at the IHOP, Day. Is that where you really live?"

"You sound crazy."

"*You* sound crazy. Why would you lie to me?" The hurt wells in my chest, pressing against my rib cage with the beat of my heart. "I'm only trying to help you, and—"

He lifts his hands in a silent plea, probably hoping I'll shut up. "Well, *Summer,* maybe you should focus on helping people who deserve it."

"What the hell are you talking about?"

"I missed the damn meeting, okay? There. That's all the proof you need. I'm not a hero. I'm just a guy trying to get a job, and what are the odds of that?"

"They're pretty good, if you must know—" I wave the papers in his face. "You *would* know if you'd shown up, but you didn't."

"That's right. I never show up. All I ever do is leave you."

"*Ding ding ding!*" I shout, my throat going tight. "You *did* leave me, after you kissed me eight years ago, and then you showed up and did it again. You kissed me and then you *left* me, and humiliated me, as if I wouldn't figure out it was an address for a fucking pancake shop."

"Summer—"

"You're despicable." There's my finger again, rising, jabbing at him. "You have no idea what you've done, how much I've thought of you, how much I—"

He grabs my wrist out of the air, wrapping it in his fingers as easily as if I'm a china doll. Half a breath and I collide with him, against the clean, spicy scent of him, the wall of muscle and pain that is Dayton Nash.

He kisses me a third time.

His hand rises to meet my jawbone, tilting my head back so that he can claim my lips for himself. It's the kiss to end every other kiss. I've never tried to straddle a man during a kiss before but I hike up my knee and press against him, need and want centered between my legs. It's not a soft kiss. It's hard and fierce and I close my teeth around his bottom lip, pulling it through, biting him like he's mine, mine, *mine.*

He lets out a low growl and his grip on my jaw tightens, his other hand locked on my ass, his mouth possessive on mine. He is all man, all thunder and force, and I am a lightning rain.

Dayton shifts his weight, rotating us slowly, finding the balance he needs to hold us upright.

The door to the exam room opens.

Out of the corner of my eye I see the doctor blink twice, then turn on his heel and get the hell out.

13

DAYTON

T HE *CLICK* of the door as it shuts behind the doctor is like Wes's hand on my shoulder eight years ago.

This time, there's no Wes to stop us.

It's *me* stopping us, and only because I'm teetering right on the edge with Summer. She tastes like sweetness and hope and I want to hear what it sounds like when I make her come. There's an exam table in here and I'd fuck her on that, honestly, I would, but that's not good enough for her. No.

Her hands are curled into my shirt, two fists wrinkling the fabric, and she sucks in a breath when I pull away.

"Want to get out of here?"

Summer's eyes are open wide, her lips slightly parted, but as my words register she gives me a sly smile. "Not a chance in hell." She drops her hands away from my shirt. "You're keeping *one* appointment today."

She flounces to the door, head held high, and while she's

calling the doctor back in I take the opportunity to adjust the unbelievable erection I got from the taste of her. More than that—from that handful of her firm ass, the way her other knee rose and hooked on my hip. How'd *she* back away from *that*? Jesus. What a smartass.

I love that about her.

It's not Dr. O'Connors I'm meeting with today, it's some prosthetic specialist. He's a short guy, reddish hair, and I can't say I hate the way he struggles to look me in the eye. I don't care what he saw. I'm still buzzed from that kiss, that mistake of a kiss, that disaster of a kiss.

"—fitted for a custom socket." I surface mid-sentence.

"Great."

He narrows his eyes. "It *is* great, Dayton. You're risking serious nerve damage, using the temporary fitting this way."

My instinct is to laugh, to brush it off. Who the hell cares if I have more nerve damage in my residual limb? My fucking *foot* is gone. But with Summer's eyes intent on me from the plastic chair tucked next to the handwashing sink, I can't do it. "I know. I get it. When can I get scheduled in for the fitting?"

We go back and forth on dates that'll fit in with Killion. "Or your new job," Summer cuts in with her professional tone. It almost sets the doctor at ease. Almost.

He presses an appointment card into my hand and leaves. The sound of my stomach growling overpowers the soft *click* of the door.

Summer stands up briskly. "Let's go."

"Back to your office?"

She shoots me a look. "No. To eat. You're always an asshole when you get hungry. And clearly—" She nods in my direction.

"You liked it."

"I liked the end."

I don't tell her how an argument with her is better than any day without her.

*****

Out on the sidewalk, Summer puts up her hood. "My place or yours?" Then she holds up a hand. "No, I won't make you take me to your *fake* place. We'll go to mine."

I want to take her to the nicest restaurant Midtown has to offer, but I can't afford that. I can't even afford a shitty place. Not with the money I owed when I got here, and the bills on top of that. Worst of all, Summer knows it. Otherwise she wouldn't be inviting me to her place. Shame trips its fingers down the back of my neck. "That's fine."

She elbows me through the thick padding of her winter coat. "You owe me one for standing me up in the first place."

When she puts it that way...

Her apartment's not far, but it's far enough that my leg aches by the time we reach the lobby of her building. I distract myself by watching the curve of her ass peek out from beneath her coat. There's not much to be seen until we're in the elevator and she shrugs it off.

Inside, she hangs her coat neatly on a hook inside the

entryway and holds out her hand for mine. "My roommate's at work," she says, as casually as she might say *that was a cold walk* or *I have to be back at one.* But she doesn't say either of those things. She lets her hips sway on the way to the kitchen and I follow her there.

She flits from the fridge to the microwave, then to the toaster. "You can have a seat, if that's more comfortable."

My missing foot has a cramp, but sitting on the high stools next to her kitchen island at least takes the pressure off the stump. "What are you making?"

"What am I *reheating*, is more like it." The toaster pops and she takes down a salt grinder from a slim cupboard up above. There is buttering involved, and then she adds the salt. Whatever it is smells delicious, but how can the food compete with the view of her body underneath her slim-cut work pants, a pale pink dress shirt on top, the outline of her camisole barely visible beneath?

"Ta-da," she says, turning to face me with two plates in her hands.

It's spaghetti.

And not gross-ass, leftover spaghetti. Delicate with red sauce like her mother used to make—that's why it smelled so familiar. She's made garlic toast.

"It was my weekend make-ahead," she says with a laugh. "It's a good thing you're here. I wasn't going to get through all of it myself."

"It's Monday."

"I have a sense for these things."

She comes around the island and puts one plate in front of me, then places her own down in front of the next stool.

"Be careful," she says automatically. "It's hot—" As she stands tall again, her breasts brush against my shoulder, the intake of her breath a whisper against my cheek.

I twine one hand around the back of her neck and pull her to me, claiming her lips for the second time today, and it's less of a battle than it was in the doctor's office. She's there, instantly there, her arms curling around my neck, legs curling around my waist, and she's panting. *Panting.*

I want my hands on every inch of her but I settle for a stroke down her waist and feel her hip rise to meet my palm. Summer throws her head back, giving me access to the soft skin of her neck. "Aren't you hungry?" she breathes.

"For you."

She shivers under my touch, and my mind wanders back to the locked door of the apartment.

We're safe here.

I can have her.

I have to have her.

Energy rushes through me and I stand up, lifting both of us off the stool, then set her on her feet. "Dayton?"

"I want to see you." I trail my thumb over her collarbone. "Show me everything."

Her eyes sparkle, tiny bursts of want glittering there, and she takes a step back. "Show *me* everything." Her voice is a little uncertain and my cock jumps in my pants

"No." I step closer, pitching my voice low. "I've been waiting years for this." I bend to speak into her ear. "And I'm not the kind of man who takes orders."

Another shiver, a soft gasp, and then Summer's hands are working at the buttons of her shirt, and then the clasp of her bra.

She's the most beautiful thing I've ever seen. The curves of her waist. Her breasts—fuck. I put my calloused hands against her hips and she tilts her head up, her nipples standing up in the cool air, and I take her mouth one more time while I circle one of those nipples with the pad of my thumb.

The sound she makes is half moan, half whimper, and it might as well be a bomb dropping against the last of my self-control.

I break the kiss and shove her pants down as far as I can reach—I can't get on my knees, not when things are moving this fast—and she scrambles to step out of them, scrambles to get back to me, desperate, grasping, and I have all of her in my hands. My sweet Summer spreads her legs and strad-dles me again, mouth furious against mine, and I balance her with one hand while I dip the other between her legs.

Her folds are soaked and at my touch the words spring out of her. "Oh, please, please..."

I am unleashed.

With a growl I can't control I turn us both. Three quick steps across the kitchen and her bare back is pressed against the eggshell blue of the wall. I haven't felt this strong in months. I have spent the last forever off-balance, my shitty prosthetic eating into my sanity, but with her weight in my hands I am grounded, powerful, rooted to the ground. My balance is *just* fine. She nips my neck and pleasure rockets down my spine and coils at the base. With one hand I undo my pants.

"Please—"

"We shouldn't do this." That's as much as I can give it. That's as much resistance as I have in my entire body.

Summer gives me a wicked grin and licks my neck. She tilts her hips. She takes me in one stroke.

The apartment falls away. The world falls away. It's her heat and wetness and nothing else—nothing but the smooth feel of her skin on mine, her muscles tightening around my cock. Harder. *Harder.* My hands on her hips, the way she braces as I fuck her.

As I come, her cries in my ears. Sinful pleasure. Angels singing, here on earth.

She's still trembling when we untangle from one another, still clinging to my neck, but she straightens up after a minute. Lifts her chin. Grins at me, her cheeks flushed and pink. "So are you—"

I bend to press my lips against the curve of her neck. "Satisfied? Never."

"I was going to say *are you still hungry.*"

"Ravenous," I whisper into her ear.

"Let's eat," she whispers back.

14

Two Years Ago

"Look at those fuckers run."

Wes sneers it out of the side of his mouth, hands loosely steering the wheel of the dust-coated Humvee. He doesn't give a shit about the little kids running through the Afghani countryside, but he should. They're the ones who know where the mines are buried. I'd rather not acknowledge him, but I'm keeping a lookout. The more eyes the better.

This deployment is stretching out into forever. Endless raids, endless missions. It's not like the planning process is any less tedious into these hours-long drives into rural villages in the foothills, our line of Humvees rumbling along at an agonizingly slow, agonizingly fucking dreary, pace. We stop a lot to question random bullshit. We take *precautions*. We mark the waypoints.

I should be happy—or at least *happier*. A month ago I got bumped to the action development team, so I get to go to planning meetings. Planning is the only thing that holds my attention, but in reality, it's as skull-numbing and terrifying as riding in the Humvee. The information we gather in those meetings gets routed up to the battalion level, and then they spend three weeks planning out where we're going to go, what we're going to do once we get there.

Or else they're just sitting on their hands. I have no idea. This was supposed to be a career for me, but I don't think I can stand it for that long. Another deployment with Wes might turn us into mortal enemies.

"What does it look like to you?"

"Hard to say."

Asshole. Of *course* it's hard to say.

"That's not what I asked."

"Can't tell."

The sides of the Humvee press in around me. Around *us*. It's suffocating. I breathe in a measured pace to keep from choking on the air. Four of us are crammed in here, with all the various shit you have to take if you're going anywhere off the base in Afghanistan. Us, and the tension. The air is thick with the relentless, unspoken tension between us, as heavy as the dust that hangs into the air and invades my lungs with every breath.

I've been off the fucking base for two weeks. It's starting to wear on me. Not that remaining on the base is a guarantee of safety. Nothing is guaranteed out here, but at least I know there aren't IEDs lying around the sleeping quarters.

If a bomb dropped on those, we'd be in real trouble. I rest easier knowing they're not buried under my bunk.

Setting Wes off is the only danger. He has my back no matter what. We're brothers-in-arms. But on American soil, he distances himself from me. No surprise. He still hasn't gotten over the *one time* I kissed his sister. I get it, on one level. My dad did not do our family reputation any fucking favors.

But I haven't lived there since junior year. Wes knows that.

"Guess."

Wes sighs. "They're kids running." His face is tanned from the constant exposure out here in the sun, but I know that under his goggles the skin around his eyes is white. I've seen more of Wes Sullivan on this deployment than I ever wanted to see in my life. I keep waiting to find out if we're still friends or just battle buddies. He'd have my back in a fire-fight—I can count on that—but the days of playing video games in his bedroom and joking around about girls are long gone. "They could be running to alert the local cell, or running because a Humvee's about to drive through downtown."

"Maybe both."

"You're absolutely right." He exaggerates a Midwestern accent. We're from New York, but it gives me a twinge of nostalgia for literally anywhere in the United States of America.

Or anywhere other than here.

"Fuck." Wes taps at the GPS unit in front of him on the dash, hard, like he's giving it a piece of his mind. "I just lost our waypoints."

This is the last backwater village we're visiting on this mission. This is the last group of civilians we're going to intimidate into naming names. The names we get are almost never worth it. I've matched up more Taliban to houses in these windswept villages than I can count. I've thrown more flashbangs into empty buildings than you want to know about.

"They're gone."

"That's what I just said, asshole."

"The kids."

The last one disappeared around the curve of a path leading into the foothills, his feet kicking up dust that rises and then settles.

"Do you have the map?"

"Ready and waiting, sir."

"Double check that next waypoint."

Another layer of sweat beads up on my neck and starts dripping down my back. I've lost count of how many times I've sweated through the t-shirt underneath my uniform. I bang my elbow against the door of the Humvee trying to open the fucking map. Wes jiggles his knuckles against the GPS unit and radios into command that we've lost it. They confirm what he wants me to do—check the paper map.

"Right up ahead."

He pulls the Humvee farther up the road—a piece of shit

dirt road in the middle of nowhere in Afghanistan. Small houses, muted gray from weather exposure, line the road. There aren't more than ten of them. Wes slows down.

Adrenaline dumps into my veins and my vision sharpens. No signs of life in this place, but that doesn't mean anything.

"Can't wait to get out of this shit."

Wes laughs into the rumble of the Humvee skirting over the dry, dusty road. He doesn't give a fuck. "Yeah. You know what Summer was telling me when I talked to her on Skype? Jesus, that computer's a mess. She said the first snow is falling at home."

I've been trying not to think about her. The mention of her name is like a hand gripping my shoulder, yanking me straight back to that kiss. The kiss and everything before that—Summer tumbling off that saucer, trying to be brave. Another bead of sweat drips down my back. It's a thousand degrees in the shade, and I miss her. "That girl loves winter. She's so fucking cute about it."

Wes whips his head around, jaw working. "What the fuck, man? How many times do I have to tell you?" He turns his head and spits onto the dirt. "That's my sister. Stay the fuck away from her."

We might as well be on the moon. Why the hell is he being such a prick about one offhand comment? "Why the fuck *should* I stay away? Explain it to me, Wes."

His smile is mocking, taunting. "Do you need a reminder? We both know this hero shit is all an act." He laughs out loud. "You're only delaying the inevitable, you criminal piece of shit."

I turn to face him, to tell him that he's done almost as many shit things as I have.

That's my mistake.

I feel it before I hear it—sheer destructive hellfire, blooming up from the wheel well right under me. I thought the sun was hot—this is a million times hotter, searing, tearing, a black smoke that tastes like gasoline and regret.

Oh fuck. *Oh fuck.*

My ears ring, the sound interrupted by shouts—that guy Powell is shouting something, his raw voice cutting in and out—and I can't tell if I'm making any sound or not. I'm choking. I'm choking to fucking death.

The pain centers into my left leg and detaches neatly from my mind, so intense I can't let it into my brain or I'll go crazy. My vision is the next to go, flickering on the edge of black oblivion. Wes was right. I don't deserve her. I don't deserve to talk about her. I don't deserve to see Summer, ever again, the way her smile lights up her blue eyes, the way that sweet smile of hers settles into something soft and willing when she's looking at me. I don't deserve to see her, and now I never will, because I was supposed to be looking for IEDs along the side of the road and I let that fucker distract me. I got distracted. I'm sorry. I'm sorry I got distracted, Summer. It's all my fault. I was thinking about you.

15

SUMMER

HAVING sex with Dayton was the biggest mistake of my life.

I shuffle a stack of papers off my desk and there he is. His *name* is there, anyway, right there spelled out in big bold letters on a folder. It's the same kind of folder I put together for all of the no-shows. Once the folder has been in the no-show pile for a month, I'll move it to a filing cabinet where he can join all the other people for whom we've previously provided services.

He's scheduled for a follow-up appointment today. In thirty minutes, actually, but I know he won't be here.

He hasn't shown up for any of his appointments over the past three weeks.

He won't answer my emails. I have no phone number, and that asshole—he never even gave me his real address. All I have is the IHOP. Do you know how desperate I am? I called the *IHOP* to see if maybe that's where he hangs out. And it's not because I'm a crazy stalker. It's because I have a lead for him. On his way out of my apartment, I questioned him about the firms he'd be most interested in working for and I submitted his resume. I have an *offer*. If he'd only show up. Or call in. *Anything*.

I'm tired.

I'm *so* tired.

It's not even ten-thirty yet.

I click over to my scheduling system and scroll aimlessly through the appointments. I can't believe he ghosted me like this. And for what?

For what?

A tear slips from the corner of my eye, hot and shameful and stupid. I'm not a crybaby. Why do I feel like such a basket case?

I get a receptionist at the VA hospital named Kathy on the line and speak in my most professional voice. "This is Summer Sullivan calling from Heroes on the Homefront."

Kathy takes in a breath and I can practically *see* her putting her hand over her heart. "Oh, you have a *wonderful* organization. Absolutely wonderful, what you're doing for these veterans."

At least the ones that show up. "That's actually what I'm calling about." I inject a note of professional concern into my voice. "One of the veterans on my caseload hasn't been showing up for appointments, and I wanted to know if you'd been experiencing the same."

"Oh, my." We're teetering on the edge of a lot of different laws here, and I know it's a long shot. "I'm not supposed to give out any information about—"

"His name's Dayton Nash," I say. "I don't want to know any private information. I *certainly* don't want to get you into any trouble. All I'm asking is—" I swallow a lump in my throat. "Has he been checking in for his appointments there?"

There's a pause, a muffled clicking sound, and then Kathy says, "Let me see, let me see." Fear and hope twist together into a knot at my core. Should I be *worried* about him? Is this about something more than Dayton being a scumbag? I can't bring myself to actually believe he's a scumbag, but if something's wrong—

"No." Kathy's voice is firm. "He hasn't checked in for any appointments since January 8."

The day we slept together.

That's not accurate. The day he pinned me up against the wall and fucked me like he'd been waiting all of his life to do it.

Which he had.

"Thank you *so* much, Kathy. I'll make a note of that." I hang up before she can say another word, dread making the bones of my wrists tingle.

"Knock, knock!"

Hazel stands in my doorway, brandishing a bright pink box. A bakery box. My stomach growls so intensely that we both hear it.

"Whoa," she says with a laugh. "I have *really* good timing. Doughnut? I picked them up fresh on my way in."

"Yes. *Yes*." I jump out of my seat and Hazel meets me halfway, holding the top of the box open.

They all look so *good*. Glazed twists. Long Johns. Classic cake with chocolate frosting and sprinkles. I hesitate between the twists and the cake doughnuts. I want that chocolate. But I want that glaze, too...

"Go ahead." Hazel clicks her tongue. "I brought more than enough for everyone to have seconds."

"You're an *angel*." I mean it. My voice wells with emotion. I take a glazed twist and one of the cake doughnuts, my heart swelling in my chest.

"I know," she says breezily. "But cool it, okay? I don't want everyone else thinking I'll always bail them out with doughnuts."

I return to my desk and devour them both, one after the other. I never eat doughnuts. I don't think about them. I don't love them. But they're both gone in a matter of bites, little slices of heaven melting between my lips. Holy *shit,* they're so good. I want more. I want a half dozen. I want a *dozen.* Two doughnuts haven't touched the pit in my stomach, or woken me up.

I'm exhausted, and it must be because of Dayton, but I can't explain the force of it. I fell asleep on the couch at seven-thirty last night. Whit woke me up at eleven and sent me to bed.

I dreamed about him.

I've seen him more in my dreams than I have in real life the last three weeks.

My frown turns to a scowl. Wes was right about him, clearly. I should have taken him at his word. Even if my brother *is* one of the world's largest assholes, he is *occasionally* right about something. I always hoped he wasn't right about Day, but—

I scroll through the schedule again. One no-show on top of another.

What a *jerk.*

I'm stricken with the powerful need for another doughnut. The craving is so powerful and urgent that it propels me right out of my seat.

Next door, Hazel has the pink box propped near the edge of her desk. I'd bet anything she means to take it down to the break room, but I'm so relieved at the sight of it I could start crying again.

The thought of which is absolutely bananas, but I brush it aside.

I knock perkily at her doorframe. "Hey, friend. Do you have any more of those doughnuts?"

If she says no, I *will* cry.

"More than half the box," she says without turning around, her fingers flying over the keyboard. "Nobody else is as hungry as you are, it seems. Take as many as you want."

"Bless you."

I approach the box with a paper napkin in hand. There is still quite a selection. God, how do I choose? *How do I choose?*

A deep red catches my eye. "Is that *red velvet*?"

"You know it is."

"I didn't even know they *made* red velvet doughnuts." I lift it out of the box. It's lighter than air, but there's a weight to it even in my hand that makes me feel almost giddy.

Then, because if Dayton is going to be like this, then screw *everything*, I reach for a glazed twist.

Hazel turns in her chair. "Girl, that's *four* doughnuts."

"I can put one—"

"Don't be ridiculous." She waves me off, laughing. "I get that way, too, when it's my time of the month."

"For *real*." I head to the door. "For real."

Only...

Only it's *not* my time of the month.

I do some quick math in my head.

That *can't* be right.

I do the math again.

Then, clutching the napkin-covered doughnuts safely in my fists, I run to check my desk calendar.

16

DAYTON

THIS ICE PACK is a piece of shit.

I press it down harder into my knee, trying to salvage every last bit of the cold that's supposedly going to cure me. That's what they said at Killion. One wrong step during a transfer. That's all it took. I saved the window. I fucked up my knee.

It's going to be a real treat going back to work tomorrow, but if I lose this job, I'll never get out of this hellhole with Curtis.

At least he's mostly sober today, and recently showered. He got a night shift job at Killion, cleaning the floors, so he can't be high all week. Sometimes that's an improvement. Sometimes it's not.

This TV show is a piece of shit, too. I don't care about British detectives, but it was on when I got here with the ice pack, my missing foot in just as much pain as my knee, and I'm not hopping around the living room to find the remote.

It's all pain since I walked out of Summer's apartment.

By choice.

That's what I keep telling myself.

It's too much of a risk for her to get involved with me. I shouldn't be fucking around with her.

My thoughts veer too close to that afternoon, and I force myself to stare harder at the TV. The volume is too loud. I wish it'd drown out the pain in my knee, in my foot, arcing across my chest, but it does nothing.

It does nothing because Summer has always been the one for me, even if it never made sense. The connection we had —fuck. It was the kind that overrides everything, even what should have been an unbreakable bond with my best friend. That piece of shit.

I ruined it all, letting my guard down in that Humvee. Maybe Wes was right. Maybe I'm a fuckup who should stay away from her, permanently. He's winning on that front. I press the ice pack down harder, though it's hardly frozen, hoping to numb the memories of finally claiming Summer, finally feeling whole again, if only for a few minutes.

A jolt of shame rushes through me, a stranglehold of panic gripping my throat so tight my vision goes black at the edges. I can't waste Summer's time. I can't ruin her life. I'm not good enough for her. I never have been, and I never will be. Staying away from her is the right thing to do.

There's a noise at the front door, but I don't turn to see Curtis going to answer. Probably one of his friends, looking for drugs.

"Day." I ignore it. He's not talking to me, unless he's mentioning something *about* me. I don't care.

"Day." His voice is closer now, next to the arm of the couch. "There's some hot chick at the door for you."

"What?"

He grins, eyes alight. "Hot chick. At the door. Asking for *you*."

"Jesus."

I wrench myself up from the couch. I can't bear to shove my stump into the prosthetic, but I do catch the ice pack before it falls to the floor. I keep it pinned to my leg while I hop for the door. My heart pounds. If it's Summer—and I don't know what other *hot chick* would be looking for me —then she's seeing this place. This place where I currently live. Fuck. It's mortifying. We're out in the direct aftermath of a party, so at least there's not open garbage everywhere, but everything is threadbare, singed somehow.

I hobble to the door, my knee pulsing with pain. It swung shut again when Curtis left, so I yank it open.

She's still standing out there.

My stomach does a double turn, and there it is—that deep at the center of my chest. I want to be closer to her. Preferably in a location that isn't this one. I don't want her to see this. There's a warmth at the center of my core. I never told her about this place. She still found it.

She turns toward me and gives a little shrug, and that's when I see them—the tears gathered in the corners of her red-rimmed eyes.

"Hey." I step out into the hallway, my gut plummeting down

to my feet. "Is everything okay?" I shrug toward the door. "I'd invite you in, but it's...not good in there."

"No need." Her voice is clipped cold. "You haven't come to any of your appointments."

"I *have* a job. You know that."

"How's that working out for you?" Her eyes flicker down to the ice pack.

I don't need this from her. I take a half-step back and end up against the door. "What are you doing here, Summer?"

"I wanted—" She swallows hard. "I wanted you to know I found a lead. One of the firms called me back on your resume, if you're still interested."

God. She's been out there, working for *me*, working to make my sad little life better, and I've been—what? Fucking myself over at the factory? The shame is like a black oil spill in my throat. The best thing I can do right now is to get her to stop wasting her time on me. That's *all* I can do.

"I'll get back to you on that." I angle myself toward the door and rest my hand on the doorknob. "Thanks for stopping by."

Hurt flashes in her eyes at the dismissal, but she lifts her chin.

"Is there something else?"

Summer looks away, at some faraway space over my shoulder. "Do you remember what we did?"

What we did *when*? I've made a lot of mistakes with her, but I assume she means the most recent one. The memory sweeps over me again—the curve of her hips as I fucked her —and it unlocks something at the center of my chest. "Yeah." She's looking at the floor again, and I ache to see her eyes. I don't think about it. I raise my hand and brush my fingertips against the line of her chin. "I remember."

Her body stiffens, her tear-brightened eyes rising to meet mine. She's repulsed. No wonder. I'm half a man who fucked her and left her behind like a piece of garbage. I reach for the doorknob again. "That was a one-time thing. Don't worry about it. I won't let it happen again."

Tears. Tears welling up in her eyes like rain, and a dull pain races from one side of my chest to the other. The emptiness of my palms is like the moment after you've dropped something precious and fragile and it shatters on the concrete.

"Sunny—"

"I also—" Her voice is strained. She tries again. "I came by to let you know that I'm pregnant."

What? Whoa.

"You don't have to do anything, but I'm keeping it." Her face flushes crimson. "At least this way I can have a part of you for myself." Her hand flies to her mouth. She didn't mean to say that last bit out loud. But she straightens up and quickly turns away, her back retreating down the hall.

I'm falling.

I catch myself on the sight of her disappearing around the corner.

"Summer!" I shout it so loudly that a muffled conversation

from the next apartment over comes to an abrupt halt. "Come back!"

I don't have my fucking prosthetic on, but I'm not going back for it now. I swing my body into motion, the ice pack falling and hitting the filthy floor with a wet *thud,* and punch one hand against the wall. I look like an idiot. Please, let her turn around—

Summer takes one step back into view as I reach the end of the hallway, and I wrap one arm around her, half for balance, half because I'm never letting her go again.

"Day—"

I brusquely gather her to me and breathe in the scent of her hair.

She could have been mine.

She could have been mine all along. I feel it in the way she relaxes in my arms, lets me hold her, even though we're technically fighting.

Summer makes a sound against my chest.

She's crying. Sobbing.

I pull her in closer to me.

I'll block out all the world if I have to.

I might be broken, but she needs me to be a man. There are no other options.

"I'm here," I murmur into her hair. "We're in this together. Sunny, it's all right."

17

SUMMER

The hallway is disgusting.

It's dirty, and the smellscape is more like decrepit mall food court than apartment building, but in Dayton's arms, all I can smell is the fresh, spicy scent of his skin. My gut rocks in a mortifying hiccup, and there's a sound like the slow leak of a faucet.

It's my own tears, hitting the front of my puffy jacket.

One side of Dayton seems heavier than the other, his weight resting more heavily on my right shoulder than my left. There's the tiniest quake at the core of him, underneath my arms. God, he works for his balance. It's not like that day in front of the Applebee's. He's not standing up tall.

That doesn't matter. What matters is that he's out here with me.

I wrap my arms tighter around the solid wall of his abs and breathe him in. I don't know if I'm crying from panic or relief. I've always wanted this. Maybe not *this* way. Maybe not in this hallway. But every heartbeat that goes by is a dream come true in miniature.

"You're a stupid *bitch*."

The voice comes from an apartment directly above us and scares the hell out of me. Dayton's arms relax. He pulls back an inch. I don't want him to. Honestly, I'd stand here forever if it meant staying in his arms.

"I'm the stupid bitch? You fucker. You're the one ruining everyone's life, and all you can think about is your own prick."

The man's voice fires back. It's too quiet to hear what he's saying, but the tone of it is pure threat.

Okay. Maybe not *forever.*

The sound of the fight gets louder, then it softens. I focus my attention where it matters: on Dayton. On the feeling of his body pressed against mine.

He uncurls one arm from my shoulders and brushes his palm over my belly, the slightest inhale, and my heart breaks. I didn't expect him to touch me like that—like I'm something worthy of awe beneath this hideous puffy coat and a scarf that probably has snot on it now.

Day stares down at my belly, his face running through emotion after emotion. I hold my breath.

He meets my eyes, his dark eyes filled with a hard determination. It's like nothing I've ever seen before. I bet Wes saw it a lot, when they were in Afghanistan.

"How—" He rests his hand on my belly and clears his throat. "How soon can I find out more about that job you were talking about?"

I laugh out loud, sucking in a big breath of the glorious, Day-scented air. "As soon as you come in to fill out the paperwork. Like I said in my emails, if you'd bothered to read them."

"Is now good?" He doesn't wait for an answer. He lets go of me, braces one hand against the wall, and swings himself into motion. He is *hopping* toward the stairs of his walk-up on one leg.

"Day. Stop."

He stops and raises his eyebrows.

"Get your leg first. And your coat. It's freezing out there."

His jaw works. "Fine."

We make our way together back to the doorway of his apartment. This time, he holds it open for me.

It's not as bad as he made it out to be.

There's a smell hovering over everything, and the paint is as beat-up as it was in the hall. It's not a place where I'd take my shoes off, and yes...when I hear his roommate whistling in another room, a shiver runs down my spine. I have the sense I've caught this place in one of its better moments.

Day hops for the couch and tosses himself down. I'm not going to stand by the doorway, alone, so I follow him inside.

He looks at me, his expression unreadable, and my heart beats faster.

This is a thousand times more intimate than fucking.

A million.

He takes the hem of his jeans in his hands and rolls them up.

We both look.

His knee is normal.

The three inches of leg below his knee are normal.

Then the leg narrows into a knobby stub and stops.

The roommate whistles in the next room. It's an oddly similar pitch to the ringing in my ears. The noise fades into the background.

It could have been worse than this.

Whatever happened to him—whatever *really* happened to him over there—could have *ended* him. The line between a leg that ends too early and a casket in the cargo hold of a plane is so thin it makes me breathless.

I could have lost him.

Dayton's prosthetic leans up against the front of the couch. He pulls it close and takes a threadbare liner from inside, rolling it over what's left of his leg. Then he eases the leg into the prosthetic, pulling it this way and that, not looking at me.

"Will you tell me about it?"

His dark gaze flickers up to mine. He knows what I'm asking. I want to touch his skin, to reassure myself that this was all the damage that was done, but it's already covered by the prosthetic.

He tugs at it again, then braces his knuckles against the fabric of the couch and stands. He meets my eyes.

"I fucked up." Dayton takes a breath. "But I'm not going to fuck up again."

18

DAYTON

"You sure you want to get in a wreck over this?"

"I'm not going to die." Summer's voice comes across tired over the speakerphone. She's been kept awake for a month, agonizing over this. I've answered every single one of her calls regardless of the time. As hard as I tried, I couldn't stop her from renting a car this morning.

"Maybe not from the snow."

She ignores this comment. "I think we can both agree that the weather is not good."

"The weather is *terrible.*"

Summer speaks in a fast and frantic voice. "What do you want me to do? Turn around? If you want me to turn around, I'll turn around."

I laugh. "You're not a good liar."

"I can turn around. If it's that hazardous, then I should do the right thing and—"

"No. You're almost there."

There's a pause, and my pulse skyrockets. I grip the phone tighter. "Summer?"

"I *have* to do this, Day. I couldn't just—"

"I know."

I shift my position from where I'm reclining on the bed in my third-floor walk-up. The whole place smells stale this morning. Summer's roommate went out of town last night, so I stayed with her. Being back in this place, after *that,* makes my skin crawl.

"I can't tell them in a phone call. It wouldn't be right."

A nervous energy prickles over my knuckles. I'm nervous *for* her. I know how they feel about me. I know how they've *always* felt about me.

"I get it." Summer's always been about *doing the right thing.* "But you don't have to tell them the whole story."

"What do you mean?" That day at her apartment flashes into my mind. The weight of her willing body in my hands. The drawn-out guttural sound she made, deep in her throat, when I took her. I don't know why I tried to leave her again after that. I'm addicted to the slick, tight feeling of my dick buried inside her.

"Maybe you don't have to tell them that I'm the father." I'm addicted to her. That doesn't mean it's right for Summer. In fact, with Alexei back in the city and breathing down my fucking neck, it *is* all wrong for Summer.

"Are you kidding me?"

"No."

"So you think I should walk in there and tell them I'm pregnant from a one-night stand and I don't know who the father is?"

I lay back on the bed. The pillow is too thin, worn through, and this conversation is making my amputated foot hurt. The tension wraps through the arch like a cramp. I can't get it to release.

"It would be better than telling them it was me."

"You really think that?" She sounds wounded, even though I'm the one who's the piece of shit.

"Yes."

"Well, I don't. And—" I can practically see her lifting her chin. "I'm not ashamed that we slept together."

"We did *way* more than sleep together," I joke, and she laughs.

"Stop. I'm trying to concentrate on the road."

"I'm going for accuracy."

"If you get any *more* accurate, I'm going to turn this car around." The desire lacing her voice; even if it's dampened by worry, sparks a matching desire at the base of my spine. I wish she'd turn around. I wish she'd leave her family out of this, but Summer's never going to do that. And I'd never ask her to.

"Last night..."

"What about it?"

I want to draw her out, erase the dark circles from under her eyes, make her laugh again.

"I've never heard you make sounds like those."

"Day," she scolds, and I know she's blushing, I know her cheeks are that deep red that makes me want to caress her face in my hands. She clears her throat. "I thought we were in this together."

"We are."

"Now you're trying to get me to turn around."

"I'm mostly kidding."

"Do you *really* want me to keep you—to keep *us*—a secret?"

A bright blaze of hope seers through my chest at the sound of her voice. "No. What I want is for you to tell your family that we're going to do this, we're going to make it, and I want them to be happy for you."

We're both silent a long time.

"I don't know if that's going to happen," she admits carefully.

"They love you," I tell her. "They might not be thrilled at first, but they're still going to love you."

"How do you know?"

"Because they're your family. They'll love you no matter what."

"You don't have to pretend that everything will be okay just because I'm pregnant with your baby."

Pregnant with your baby makes me hard as a rock. The thought of her belly getting round with *my baby* is so fucking sexy.

It's sexy and terrible, because being with me is a risk for her on every level. She could lose her family over this. I take a breath and try to calm the fuck down.

"Fine. I won't. It could blow up in your face."

"I know," she says softly.

"It won't," I tell her.

"I'm getting off the highway," she says abruptly. "I'll call you when I'm done."

19

"What kind of trouble are you in?"

Wes leans lazily against the doorway between the living room and the front entry, his hand wrapped around a cold beer. He's here for the weekend, too. My heart squeezes thinking of the nights Day used to spend here, back when things were simple.

"I'm not in trouble." I raise my chin defiantly and my mom sighs.

Wes smiles at me. "It's written all over your face, Sunny."

I bite back the urge to call him an asshole. We've been drifting apart ever since the dance, but that day at Applebee's made it ten times worse. It's not like I can completely cut him off, though. He's completed too many deployments. If something happened to him and we weren't speaking—

My parents sit close together on the loveseat across from my chair, holding hands. My mom bites her lip, worry written in the lines creasing across her forehead. But this doesn't *have* to be a disaster. They might not like it, but it doesn't have to be a disaster. There's a warmth deep down in my belly. I can't feel the baby moving yet, but he or she is there.

"This is all wrong." I stand up from the chair and Wes laughs at me. "Can you guys just—" I motion for my parents to stand. "I feel like we're at some weird business meeting. Or a jury trial."

My dad laughs, and unlike when Wes spoke up, his voice is warm. "Sunny, you're giving us all a heart attack. Say what you need to say."

"Are you moving out of the state?" Mom's voice is anxious. "If you are, I can understand that, but—"

"No, Mom."

"Are you sick?"

"Mom—"

"She's pregnant," Wes says from his spot at the door.

There's a stunned silence, and then Wes bursts out laughing.

"I'm just kidding." He forces the words out through his laughter and slaps his knee. "Wanted to break the tension. Did I do it?"

I glare at him, then turn my attention back to my parents. They chuckle half-heartedly, my mom's hand raised to her chest.

I take a deep breath.

Get it over with.

"Wes is right."

Dead air.

Maybe they didn't hear me.

"I'm pregnant."

My mom's mouth drops open. My dad freezes, head cocked to the side, as if I've just spoken in another language.

"I'm due in October, and—"

"Oh, my God!" My mom's shriek is ear-splitting, and I jump, my body startling at the sound. "Are you *serious*?"

"Yes." I take a step cautiously back toward the chair. "Are you—?"

"Sunny!" She leaps forward, crossing the room in two single bounds, and folds me in her arms. "Sunny, oh, my God. Pregnant!" She kisses me on the cheek and pulls me in for another hug. "Robert, I'm going to be a grandmother!" Mom backs up and takes my hands in hers, eyes shining with the start of tears. "I can't believe it. Oh, I can't believe it." Her expression flies into one of deep thought. "I want to be called Nana. No, Mimi. Or maybe just Linda."

"What—" The relief coursing through my veins is so strong that I feel like I'm about to pass out. She's *excited*. I scan the room—Dad looks confused, and Wes is stone-faced. After a second, Wes nods, straightens up, and walks assuredly over to me. He pats me awkwardly on the shoulder.

"We'll be here for you, Sunny," he says gruffly. "Whatever you need. You can call anytime."

"You can," insists my mom. "Oh, please let me babysit for

you. I would *love* that. I'm sure you're going to need a lot of help. Robert, do you think we could pitch in for some daycare? I can't take the baby every day while you're at work, but we could help out with the cost." She squeezes my hands. "You'll want a great place. It's so important. But don't worry, honey. We'll be there for you every step of the way. Do you need anyone to go to appointments with you?"

I shake my head under the barrage of her words.

They think I'm going to be a single mom.

I guess I *could*. I guess things *could* turn out that way, but Day said he'd be there for me. He's been there for me already. He sat in the room with me for the first ultrasound. He answers the phone every time I call, unless he's on the floor at the factory. But I'm not going to give voice to that inkling of doubt at the back of my mind. Not a chance.

"Uh—" I squeeze my mom's hands back and take a deep breath. "I'm okay on the appointments, actually. The father —he's involved."

There's a shift in the room. Mom takes a step back. "He is? Why isn't he here with you?"

"He—he didn't think he should come. This time." I hate being this cryptic, but now that the time has come, I can hardly get the words out. "Because—"

"Who'd you sleep with, Sunny?"

My mom shoots Wes a look of pure poison. "You can be honest with us, okay? Even if you don't know who the father is."

"Oh, my God." I rub a hand across my forehead. "I *know* who the father is." I don't look at Wes. "It's Dayton."

Mom's hand goes to her mouth. "You met another Dayton?"

"You've got to be fucking kidding me," Wes thunders.

"Son—" My dad's tone is warning.

Wes turns on his heel and stomps upstairs, his feet thudding on every step.

"It's Dayton Nash, Mom." I look into her eyes. I will not feel ashamed about this. There's no reason *to* feel ashamed about this. "He's back in the city. We've been seeing each other." This is true. We have been. We might not have a *title*, but...

"That's good," Mom says warily. "That's good." She turns back toward my dad, then looks back at me. "Listen," she says softly. "Honey, are you sure that he's the right man to—"

"He's the *perfect* man," I tell her, my voice rising. "And if you're going to act like that, then there's no need for me to—"

"Sunny." She cuts me off, stepping back in for another hug. "I only want you to be happy."

"I'm *so* happy, Mom." My throat goes tight saying the words. "I'm so happy."

20

COME OVER.

The text comes in early, just past nine in the morning on Sunday. Summer didn't have much to say when she called yesterday. She was vague, distant.

I run a hand through my hair. I was dreaming when the phone buzzed. Something about a hospital. I couldn't find her. It was fucking terrible.

Right now?

Right now.

I throw myself out of bed and feel around for the prosthetic. My leg still burns from yesterday. I worked a couple over-time hours at Killion. It's my last week at the place, but I need all the money I can get. My skin paid the price.

I shove my leg into it and take a flannel shirt from the end of the bed. If Summer wants me over there, I'll go. My gut twists into a cold, heavy knot.

This can't be good news.

I⊤'s FRIGID, freezing, and Summer is bundled up in a hoodie and thick sweatpants when I get to her apartment. It's silent and gray inside, reflecting the cloudy day. She doesn't say anything as I step inside.

"Whitney's coming back for brunch," she says finally, once the door's locked behind us.

"Okay." Whitney's one of those people who is so fucking enthusiastic, it's exhausting to be around her. Summer loves her.

"I'm going to tell her what's happening."

"That's good," I say carefully. "I think you should."

She looks up at me, defiance written on her face. "I also think we should decide what we're going to do."

"About the baby?"

"About us."

"Sunny—"

"Don't say my name like that," she says sharply. "I got up at the asscrack of dawn to get back here and talk to you about this in person. It was *snowy*."

I stifle a laugh. She looks so pissed about the snow, but it's not really about the snow. It can't be.

"I know you hate driving in the snow, so I appreciate it."

"Well, I appreciate knowing what's going to happen."

I put a hand on the line of her jaw and tilt her face up toward mine. "Summer."

"Yeah?"

"What is it you want to talk about? I'll talk about anything you want."

Her mouth presses into a thin line. "I told my parents we were seeing each other."

"We are." I grin in spite of myself. "We've seen a lot of each other."

That's when I see it—the fear in her eyes, and the hope. "What are—" She clears her throat. "What are your plans, then?"

She's not asking about the baby. I've promised her we're in it together when it comes to the baby. She's asking about something else entirely.

It's a rush of emotion, a storm cloud breaking apart over me so powerfully that the pain in my leg pulses to match it.

I can't *really* be with her...but I want to.

I want her to be mine so much that I'm willing to put her in harm's way. I shouldn't fucking do that.

No. The thought is loud and clear. *You're protecting her. This is the best way to protect her, and you.*

"I hope you know how—" I'm lost for words, and Summer's eyes fill with tears. She starts to turn away and I catch her by the elbow. "Sunny, that's not it."

"What is it, then?"

"I was hopeless without you."

Her eyes widen.

"I was fucking hopeless. I'm—" I gesture at my leg. "I'm... fucking broken."

"You're not," she protests.

"I didn't see any way out of a shitty existence. But when I saw you at that office—" I shake my head. This is getting sappy as fuck, and I don't care. "I felt hopeful for the first time in a long time."

She raises one eyebrow. "Is that why you tried to avoid me?"

There it is—that dread. "I tried to avoid you because I'm a risk."

She scoffs.

"No. My life is a risk. I have things from my past that—that aren't resolved."

"Another woman?" Her voice cracks on the word.

"No. Nothing like that." A solution is dawning in my mind. Why the hell didn't I think of it before? Oh, because I was wallowing in the pain. Always the pain. Every day, every night. "I'm just warning you, Sunny, that I've been around some rough people."

"I don't care," she says, defiance lighting up her face.

"They might not be done with me yet."

"I'll protect you," she says, and laughs.

"But I want to be with you."

Her shoulders slump with relief. "And not because I'm pregnant?"

"Oh, Jesus, Sunny, I wanted to be with you *years* ago."

She pouts. "Why didn't you?"

"There were mitigating circumstances."

"Wes," she says instantly. "That asshole."

"He might have had a point."

"He's never had a point in his life." Summer's face goes red. "He's always been wrong about you."

I take her in my arms and wait. She looks up into my eyes and her body goes still and calm. Trusting. "I want you to make the best choice for *you*."

"I want you to realize I'm an adult woman."

I laugh. "Trust me. I *know* you're an adult woman." My cock jumps at the thought of her naked body stretched out on the sheets beneath me. "But if it's too dangerous—"

"I want to be with you, Day." She swallows hard. "Please. If you don't want the same thing, tell me now."

"Hey, Summer," I say casually, like we're walking down the hall in our old high school.

"What?"

"Will you be my girlfriend?"

"I don't know," she says, and then giggles. It's the fucking cutest thing I've ever seen. "I might be too *dangerous* for you to—"

I silence her with a kiss. Her lips are warm and soft and willing, and I flick my tongue between them, testing. She opens her mouth and lets me in. By the time I release her, she's panting. "Are we together now, then?"

"Fuck yes," I say.

Summer gives me a wicked look. "Then make me yours."

"I have news."

Whitney clears her throat, then wraps her slender fingers around her martini glass.

I give her a look. "What are you doing?"

"Preparing to toast you."

"You don't even know what I'm going to say."

"Yes, I do," she says smugly. "You're going to tell me that you have a new boyfriend. A *hot* boyfriend. Named Dayton Nash."

"That's part of it," I admit.

She raises the glass in the air. "Ladies and gentlemen," she says loudly, interrupting everybody at the nearby tables. "My best friend Summer has at last, *at last*—"

"Stop," I hiss at her.

She lowers the glass. "What? This is cause for celebration, isn't it?"

"Yes," I say, blushing furiously. "But there's—there's more."

"Oh, my God." She puts the glass down on the table with a hard *clink*. "You're leaving me."

"Maybe eventually, but that's—"

"I can't believe you would leave me for a *man*. Summer, we have a perfect arrangement. Our apartment is lovely. Our friendship has never been stronger. I pull you out of your goody two-shoes shell and make sure to feed the part of your soul that needs a good party, and—"

"Whit—"

"—you would throw all that away for Dayton Nash? He's hot, but he's not *that* great. He lives in Queens, for one thing, and that's—"

"Whitney."

"—that's too far to commute, which means that if you move to Queens, we'll never see each other again. How am I supposed to live my life if you're—?"

"I'm pregnant."

"*What*?!" Her shriek is so loud, it stops all the traffic at the restaurant.

"I'm pregnant." I'll admit—saying it out loud brings me a ridiculous pleasure.

Whitney's eyes might as well be saucers. "Is it *his*?"

"Jesus, Whit, *yes*, it's his."

She leans back in her chair, closes her eyes, and fans herself with her hand. "How did it happen? Tell me every detail."

"I got pregnant. From having sex."

She keeps fanning. "It wasn't just *sex*, was it? It was hot. It was furious. I bet those big hands of his—"

"We are *not* talking about this in a restaurant." Not that I'll ever describe to her the perfect length of Day's cock, or the way his thickness is exactly right for me, or the way the head hits my g-spot when he— "We're not."

"Was it on the floor?"

"No."

"Was it in—?"

"Whitney. Celebrate with me. I'm pregnant."

She raises her glass again, but I can see a sheen of tears in her eyes. "A toast to you and your future baby," she says, her voice shaking a bit. "I'm happy for you, Sunny."

I sigh a little and raise my water glass. "But you're sad, too."

"Well, *yeah*. You're the best roommate ever. You even do the dishes."

"I do the dishes because it's the right—"

"—thing to do," she finishes for me. Then she takes a deep, cleansing breath and digs into her purse for her phone. "Give me your mother's number."

"Why? What for?"

Whit looks at me like I was born on another planet. "We have to start planning your baby shower." She waggles her eyebrows. "It's going to be *epic*."

22

THE RECEPTIONIST AT GLOBAL CONNECT, Inc. smiles up at me from behind her desk. "Good morning, Mr. Nash. It's finally starting to warm up out there, don't you think?"

I scan my access card through the reader next to her desk. An access card. Through the reader. It's a far cry from walking in past the foreman at Killion, who would stand there with his arms crossed, looking at everybody like we were late for a prison shift, even if we were ten minutes early.

Christine's right. "It could be a little warmer. It's almost April."

She laughs as if this is the funniest thing anyone has ever said and waves me in.

I play it cool, like working in an office is a normal thing for me to do.

It should be normal, after almost a month on the job, but it still seems fucking crazy to me that I'm here at all. GC, even with the most ridiculously generic name I've ever heard for a company, isn't the kind of place I ever dreamed I'd work at. It's boring as hell to explain to another person, but basically, we're a go-between for charities and nonprofits and the places they serve. Somebody has to arrange for shipping massive amounts of lifesaving crap all over the world. That's us. It takes so much planning, it makes mission development look like target practice—too easy.

The hero's welcome isn't my *favorite* thing, but other than that—

"Good *morning,* Dayton." Susan stands up from her desk to greet me. "How are you?" She's in her sixties, silver-haired and poised, and she looks at me every morning like I've just shipped home from the front lines with a shiny medal pinned to my chest.

"I'm all right. How are you, Susan?"

"Very well. *Very* well, thank you." She nods to herself—a job well done—and sits back down in her seat.

"Liar." Simon. Good old Simon. He's the only one in this place who doesn't worship me so much that he's afraid to joke. Conveniently, he has the cubicle across the way from mine, so he has plenty of opportunities.

I hang my coat up on the hook by my chair and swivel to face him. "Who says?"

"Your face says." He waggles his eyebrows. "Rough night?"

I rub my hands over my face. Yes, there's grit in my eyes and a heaviness at the corner that only coffee will dispel—hopefully—but as far as rough nights go, I've had worse. "No."

"Shut up. You're *totally* hungover."

I wish. "I'm not."

"You can admit it to your old buddy Simon." He stands up, his own mug of coffee still steaming, and leans against the doorway of my cubicle. "Come on. Your girlfriend's *gorgeous.* It's okay to say you were up all night *pleasing* her, and—"

"If by *pleasing her* you mean holding her hair back from her face when she throws up. She's pregnant and sick as hell."

The expression on his face changes from teasing to serious and fatherly, even though we're the same age. "Shit, dude. Yeah. My wife was sick all nine months." He shakes his head. "I don't know why they call it morning sickness when it lasts all day."

"Yeah."

Simon perks up. "It's the most incredible thing, though, when you see that baby for the first time. All your feelings change in an instant, and—"

I want him to go away. I want to go into the break room and make an inappropriate amount of coffee, then come back to my desk in silence, get the weight off my prosthetic. It'll be easier to be excited about holding the baby when Summer isn't so obscenely sick all the time.

Simon goes on and on about the miracle of holding your child, the words nothing more than a faint buzzing sound in my ears. Her face was pale this morning when I left—she called sick into work. She can't sit in a chair in the office all day, feeling like that, but I know she hates to take time off. Sunny wants to be there.

So do something about it.

"—and when they laugh...God, it's—" Simon looks rapturous.

I clear my throat. It's not that I *want* to ask him these things, but if he knows something that'll help Summer, I'll admit defeat. "What'd you do to help her? Your wife?"

His eyes light up at the chance to share more insight. "Those Club crackers? I always kept a box by her bed. She'd eat a few of those before she got up in the morning—I mean, literally, before she even sat up, and that would help. Plus, they make these suckers out of herbs or some magic shit. Should have bought stock in those. Ginger ale, too. She carried around a tumbler with a straw in it for months. I got so sick of washing that thing."

I'd wash a tumbler every five minutes if it would help her feel better.

Simon raises his coffee mug in a salute. "Good luck, man. Try some of that stuff out."

"I will. Thanks." This is the part where, at Killion, the other guy would give me endless shit about getting a girl knocked up, where he'd bring some other people into it, where it would become an all-day shitfest, until somebody threatened a fight. Simon only goes back to his cubicle and sits down in his chair.

It feels like cheating, working in a place like this.

"Hey, Nash?" He sticks his head out from behind the wall of his cube.

"Yeah?"

"Congratulations."

Pride loops its way through my chest. "Thanks."

I write down his list of recommendations on my notepad.

It's nothing but meetings and phone calls and shuffling paper until after lunch, until that three o'clock lull that doesn't exist at factories like Killion. You work until the bell rings at the end of your shift. You don't fuck around at three in the afternoon, recovering from an afternoon slump.

Not that I'm fucking around.

I go on Amazon and search out everything that Simon was talking about, except the ginger ale and crackers—I'll get that at the bodega on the way home. The lollipops look weird, but I don't care. I find a tumbler shaped like a Starbucks cup, only with a straw, a delicate snowflake pattern on the edge. Perfect. I add a misting spray meant to help with morning sickness and a relaxing candle to the order. I'll draw a bath for Sunny, if that's what she wants.

Everything's loaded up. I pick the fastest shipping method and dig my wallet out of my pocket. I have a credit card for the first time in my life. It's a small miracle. Summer has no idea how good it feels to pay for these things for her. I guess she's been doing it on her own all along.

The phone on my desk rings before I can punch in the credit card numbers and I answer it without looking at the caller ID. "Dayton Nash."

"It's so sexy when you say your name like that."

Summer.

"Like I'm answering the phone at an office building?"

"Like a workin' man who's wearing a button-down shirt..." Her voice trails off at the end of the sentence, almost wistfully. "That I could unbutton..."

"You are a *sucker* for business casual."

"I can't help that you wear it so well." She's teasing, but I know she's half-serious. Summer loves taking my shirt off at the end of the day. She loves doing more than that.

I press the big yellow *order* button on the screen and watch the browser load the confirmation screen. "How are you feeling?"

Summer sighs, a little sound that could be relief or frustration—it's different, day to day. "Better."

"Are you sure?"

She groans. "Now it's the opposite. I could eat for *days*. I'm so hungry, Day. I'm *starving*. And work keeps forwarding messages from my desk phone. The last one was just some guy who said my name and then breathed through his mouth. It was *disgusting*. And still, I'm so hungry, I could die." The last bit is so dramatic, I can picture her swooning onto a fainting couch.

"I'll make dinner tonight."

"Okay, but *how much* dinner?"

"All the dinner the two of you can eat." She laughs. "And if that's not enough, I'll go out for more. How does a second dessert sound?"

"Almost as good as unbuttoning that shirt."

Simon glances over at me from his cubicle and gives me a

thumbs up. Yeah. Time to end this call. I twist toward the inner corner of my own cubicle and lower my voice. "You can unbutton it all you want in two hours."

"Come *straight* home," Summer says. "This apartment is too empty without you."

Who could resist *that* kind of invitation?

23

SUMMER

THE LOLLIPOP IS a burst of sour—sour *something*—on my tongue. "Oh, my God."

Dayton rolls over in bed, his face creased from the pillow, and pushes himself halfway up. "Are you okay?"

I brandish the lollipop in his face. "What *is* this?"

He reaches over me to grab for the box on the bedside table and consults it, dark eyes lit up with an amusement that makes me feel a warm blush of pleasure, despite the disgusting puke feeling threatening from the edge of the bed. "Looks like sour raspberry."

"Yikes."

Still, I take another lick of it.

Dayton tosses the box back onto the bedside table and swings his legs over the side of the bed. He hops for the bathroom. Water runs.

I lick the lollipop again. It's not *terrible,* but it is *really* sour.

They're not kidding about that part. And the rocking, seasick feeling in my gut is subsiding, at least a little. It's worst when I've just woken up.

I need to get more of it in my mouth.

"Christ." Dayton leans against the doorway of the master bath, his dark eyes on me.

I raise a hand to my hair. "That bad, huh?"

He grins, a half-smile that has warmth going *other* places, and leaps for the bed. "That bad." Under the covers, he runs one hand over the curve of my belly, lifting beneath the tank top. I look more food baby than actual baby, but my tank top doesn't care about the difference. It was a little small when I bought it. Now we're over the line. "Your tongue on that thing—"

"You *bought* this for me. One-day shipping!" I shake my head. The box showed up yesterday afternoon and Dayton tore into it, lifting out each item one at a time, convinced it would cure me.

So far, he's been right.

He kisses my neck and his hand slides down, finding the elastic of my panties and slipping beneath. "I didn't think it would be so sexy to watch you eat them."

"Day—" The last blurry edges of the nausea dissipate when he strokes my clit with the pads of two fingers. "I can't—" I should brush my teeth. It's time for my workout. If I don't get my workout in early, I end up napping instead. Pregnancy is a bitch that way.

Everything else? Not a bitch.

Especially Dayton's fingers against my clit, his lips teasing the line of my jaw, his voice in my ear. "You can."

I relax against the pillow, my eyes fluttering shut. He plucks the lollipop out of my hand and I hear the stick clatter against my empty water glass. "My workout—" It's a weak protest, and he knows it. In fact, by taking off my tank top, he's only helping me toward my goal.

"I'll make your heart beat faster, if that's what you want." His fingers move lower, playing at my entrance. "Look—you're already wet." He presses them inside, taunting me, and takes them away.

"You can't do that." It's not a whine, but it's a near thing.

"I can."

He moves over me and I open my eyes to follow the lines of his tattoos. Day's arms work—there go my panties—and then his big hands are on my thighs, spreading me open beneath him.

His eyes rake over me, possessive of every naked, exposed inch of my skin. The heat in his eyes is enough to make me come.

He must sense it, because he looks at me and strokes the inside of one thigh. "You're panting."

Desire spikes through my core. I'm getting slicker by the second. There's that grin again. Dayton commenting on my body this way turns me on like nothing else in the world.

"I want you." It's a raw whisper.

"I can see that."

I tilt my hips upward in his hands. "Please—"

He moves backward on the bed and bends his head. The first stroke of his tongue against my slit has my fists curling into the pillowcases. The second has me trembling against his lips.

"You're the sweetest thing I've ever tasted." His breath is hot between my legs, and then he can't say anything more.

I SPRAWL BACK against the pillows, freshly fucked and glowing.

Dayton nudges one arm. "Aren't you going to work out?"

"No. I'm going to stay in bed the rest of the day. That was—" I'm at a loss for words. *Transcendent* seems almost enough, but not *quite.* "That was incredible."

"Hmm." His voice is full of faux disappointment. "I'll do better next time."

I push myself up on one elbow. "Better than incredible?"

"If it was *that* incredible, you'd be on your knees, begging for more." He works his face into something resembling a hard look.

My laughter is interrupted by my cell phone, ringing on the bedside table. I snatch it up while Day falls back against his own pillow, rolling his eyes to the ceiling.

The name on the caller ID makes my stomach turn over.

It's Wes.

I haven't breathed a word of moving in with Dayton. I haven't told anyone. I like the feeling of this secret, happy bubble we're in too much to shatter it by opening my big mouth.

But I do answer the call.

"Hey, Wes. What's up?"

"Sunny," he says, his voice ringing with confidence. "I'm coming to the city next weekend. Can I take you out to lunch?"

Dayton has perked up at the sound of Wes's voice, and my heart pounds. It's not right to keep this to myself forever. It'll hurt Wes—it'll hurt *everyone*—if the first news they hear is of the birth. I owe my family some notice. I might as well start with Wes. "You know what?" I say the words slowly, choosing them one by one. "I have a new place."

"You do?" There's a rustling sound on the other end of the line like he's transferring his phone from one shoulder to the other. "I didn't know you moved."

"I did. A few weeks ago. Why don't you come over for dinner?"

I raise my eyebrows at Dayton, asking his permission. Begging his forgiveness, really. His eyes flash, but he nods, one motion. Crisp. Accepting.

"I'll be there," Wes says. "Two o'clock on Saturday?"

"Sounds perfect." I give him the address.

"See you then."

I drop the phone back onto the bedside table and look at

Dayton, who's staring back up at the ceiling. "Are you okay with this?"

He lets out a long breath, then rolls toward me, his hand coming down softly on my lower back. Day leans in and kisses me on the temple. "You should get your workout in before you get tired."

IT's the first day of April, sunny and warm for once, and my capris still fit. I'm ten days into my second trimester. Tank, bra, hoodie, I'm good to go.

I head out in front of our apartment. It's a two-bedroom in Bed-Stuy, which means a longer commute, but the neighborhood has more trees. I like how the spring sunlight filters through them.

I feel so good in this moment that I could jog. I put in one of my headphones, leaving the other one out for safety, and run down the block, slow but steady. It feels amazing to move. This pregnancy thing has made it *very* touch and go when it comes to exercise, but in my limited Googling, I learned that working out is essential to a healthy pregnancy, so I'm going to do it, damn it.

Four blocks down, during my first walking break, a car pulls up to the curb alongside me.

I dismiss it as a cab at first, but it continues rolling along next to me.

The window comes down.

"Summer Sullivan. Hey! Summer Sullivan. I see you."

It's not a voice I know. The hairs on the back of my neck stand up. The earphone closest to the car is the one that's in, so I pretend not to hear.

"Where's Dayton these days?" It's a rough voice, tinged with an accent so faint I can't place it. I'm four blocks from home. The car is here beside me. Dayton's not. "I know you know where he is."

I risk a glance at the car, but I can't see the person inside— the sun's too bright, the windows darkened, and the interior too shadowy.

I break into a run. There's a park half a block up the street. If I can get there, I'll double back. Behind me, the car screeches out into the street and the engine revs as it speeds up to stay with me. Someone behind him honks. I get to the intersection, look once, and go across against the sign. Shit, shit, *shit*. What's *happening?*

There's a young couple on the far side of the park, and I veer in the front entrance, blood singing in my ears. Is he going to get out and follow me in? The sidewalk is rough, pieces jutting up from the ground, and my heart is beating out of control. I wrench my head around—how much time do I have?—and my toe catches on a piece of concrete.

I trip and fall awkwardly to the side, landing against a concrete planter that connects with my pregnant belly. It lurches with pain. I sit down hard on the grass, nausea rising, and throw up next to the planter. I don't see anyone coming after me, and the couple is gone.

Oh God. Oh God, oh God.

24

DAYTON

It's a shitty thing to do, to blindside Wes like this. No matter how I turn it around in my head, it sucks. If it was me, I wouldn't want to walk into this nice family dinner only to find my oldest enemy sitting across from me at the table.

Summer's out jogging, and I'm standing here in the shower, trying to plan my way out of being an asshole.

Before I saw her face in that office building that day, I didn't care about being an asshole, which is why all that shit happened after my discharge. It said "honorable."

I'm not honorable.

At least, I wasn't then.

I haven't heard anything more about Alex. Alexei, I remind myself for the thousandth time. It's been a couple of months, at least. Maybe he's left the city again. I wouldn't put it past a guy like him to drop by, wreak some havoc, and then disappear. He wants me to be on edge. I'm not going to give him the pleasure.

The dinner with Wes seems more pressing.

I'm washing the scent of Summer off of me—it's a fucking shame, watching it go down the drain with the soap—when everything running through my head comes to a screeching halt. My thoughts are interrupted mid-sentence by a sound that's barely audible over the hiss of the hot water, the cascade against the floor of the shower.

The buzz of my phone.

I run my hands through my hair and turn off the water. I reach the phone before it stops ringing, but honestly, I'm glad Summer's not here to see me hop like that—frantically, trying to wrap a towel around my waist with one hand. I know exactly what she'd say. Something wildly inappropriate to entice me to get back into bed with her. As if she needs to *say* anything to entice me back into bed.

I snatch the phone up fast enough to see that it's not a number I have saved. I don't have a lot of numbers saved. Summer and I got the phones together last month, our first bill together. She let me have my name on the account. She *also* got herself a shiny new iPhone. I insisted on getting last year's model.

"Hello?" I lean my bad leg against the bed and tie on the towel. I know the people on the phone can't see me. It doesn't matter.

"I'm looking for Dayton Nash."

"This is Dayton Nash."

"Mr. Nash, I'm a nurse on staff in the emergency department at Woodhull. Your wife was brought in about twenty minutes ago for—"

I don't hear what she says. There's a rushing sound in my ears, a seizing pressure in my chest. It doesn't matter. I'm already in motion, hopping for the closet. I lean against the door and yank out boxers, jeans, and a t-shirt and throw them onto the bed.

"What's the address?"

"Sir, I want to give you the information you're going to need—"

"Stop talking and tell me the address." It's the kind of tone I used a thousand times in the military. This nurse is working in the closest thing civilians have to a war zone. She knows authority when she hears it.

Or maybe she knows it's thinly disguised panic.

Either way, she tells me the address.

Exactly one minute later, I run out of the apartment, no jacket, only my phone and wallet and that address on a sticky note. I don't even lock the door.

THE ULTRASOUND ROOM is so dark I can't see *shit* at first.

All I see is that everyone startles when I burst through the door. It's flashes of motion at the corner of my eyes and I sweep the room, eyes on every corner, once, twice. It's an old habit. I keep looking for details even as my pupils adjust to the darkness.

"Summer?"

Summer's bed in the emergency room—it has to be the

worst emergency room in the city—was empty when I got here, and you'd better fucking believe I wasn't going to wait around for her to get back.

My breathing is steady, but my heart is racing.

The ultrasound tech turns, the dim light from the machine giving her face an eerie glow. "Sir, you can't be in here."

Footsteps in the hallway. The nurse who's been trailing me all the time comes in, out of breath. "God," she says, clapping a hand to her chest. "I don't know how you can move that fast with—" She registers the look on the tech's face, which says *call security*. "This is the father. He insisted."

"Day, I'm right here."

Summer's voice is soft, and I hear the hint of a tremble, and fuck everybody else in this room. I cross over to the side of her bed and gather her into my arms. Her hoodie is hiked up over her belly and there's a paper sheet tucked into her capris. All of her is smeared with ultrasound gel.

I take her face in my hands. She looks *okay*. Shaken, but okay. She gives me a little nod.

Pain spikes up through my prosthetic. The adrenaline kept it at bay until this moment, but it's a raw, twisting pain. Summer doesn't need to know about it. I sit down heavily on a stool next to the bed and entwine my fingers through hers.

The ultrasound tech clears her throat. "Are we okay to resume the ultrasound?"

"Yes," Summer says. "Yes." Her grip on my hand tightens, and another silvery thread of adrenaline courses through my veins. What's wrong with the baby?

The tech presses the wand against her belly, swiping it back and forth until the baby emerges.

At first, all I see is a blob, but then the features resolve themselves—a tiny alien head, and—holy shit. *Fists.* Fists punching at the air.

"Here's baby," the tech says neutrally. Summer's holding my hand so tight I think she's cutting off the blood flow. More swiping of the wand, more careful examination. "*Very* active," the tech announces, after what feels like a thousand years. "I don't see any evidence of bleeding. Your baby is perfectly healthy."

Summer lets out a strangled sob and turns to bury her face in my arms.

The tech stands up, wipes off Summer's belly with a towel, and turns off the machine. "I'll give you a few minutes." She hits a switch on the way out and lights—dim, soft lights—rise in the room.

I can finally see her clearly.

Summer's hair is disheveled, pulled to one side, and I smooth it away from her face, before wrapping my arms around her. I hold her until her shoulders stop shaking.

"God," she says, sitting up and pulling her hoodie back down. "I was so scared."

I take her hand. "Sunny, why? What happened?"

Her chin trembles again and she takes a deep breath. "I was running."

"Did you fall?"

"Yes, but—" She shakes her head. "I was a few blocks away, almost to that park, and a car pulled up next to me. Some guy inside was calling out my name." Summer shivers. "My *full* name. I tried to ignore him, but then he started asking about you. Asking where you were. He said, *I know you know.*"

Oh, Jesus.

"What did he look like?"

"I didn't see him." She raises one hand to her hair, looking down. "I tried to look, but—" Her eyes meet mine, wide and regretful. "I was fucking terrified. I ran into the park and my foot caught on, I don't know, a piece of concrete? I hit a planter on the way down. Right in the belly." She winces. "Who do you know that would be looking for you?"

I gather her up in my arms and stroke her hair absently.

I know exactly who'd be looking for me, and I know why.

I never thought he'd come back for his revenge. Not like this.

I was wrong.

And now he's found us.

"Don't worry about it, Sunny. Don't worry for a second."

She wraps her arms around me and holds on tight. "Day?"

"Yeah?"

I brace for an argument, even as my mind races through all the possible options for keeping her safe. We could move out of the city. No. She'd never do that. She'd never leave Heroes on the Homefront. We could move somewhere else *in* the city. But Summer's not in any shape to apartment hunt. Not again. Last time was hard enough, and in the end, we basically lucked into the place in Bed-Stuy.

"Can we get out of here? This place is awful."

"Of course." I help her up off the bed, my mind racing. I don't want to stay at the house tonight, but I don't want to stress her out. That would be the worst thing.

I smile at her like my past isn't slashing its way into the present. "You know what I think we need?"

"What?" Summer leans her head against my arm.

"A little vacation."

She shakes her head. "We can't afford that."

"We *can*," I say, repeating our word game from this morning. God, it was just this morning.

She squeezes my hand in agreement.

25

MY HANDS TREMBLE on the pan of garlic bread, and the corner bangs against the front of the stove.

Day is instantly in the doorway of the kitchen. "Are you okay?"

"Yes, and the garlic bread survived, too."

He steps up behind me and kisses the back of my neck. "You sure you're okay?"

I lean into his strong, solid body and try to shake off the nerves. "I want this to go well."

He laughs, almost a snort. "What, you think he's going to be happy to see me?"

"Of *course* he'll be happy to see you."

"You're so cute when you lie."

"Eventually. *Eventually* he'll be happy to see you."

"That's my girl."

Dayton's sitting at the table in the kitchen when the knock comes on the door. Wes always knocks three times—loud and obnoxious and powerful. Today's no different.

I take in a deep cleansing breath and open the door.

There he is, in jeans and a black hoodie, his posture as straight as if he's in formation in the Army. It doesn't matter that he's trying to look relaxed. "Hi, Wes."

His smile is crooked now, for reasons we've never talked about, but it seems genuine enough. "Hey, Sunny." Wes wraps one arm around my shoulders and pulls me in for a hug. The nerves rise in my throat, suspiciously similar to morning sickness. I swallow it down.

Wes steps inside and kicks off his shoes, and the pressure in my ears can't wait anymore.

"Nice place, sis. I can't believe you didn't tell me before you moved in."

"Wes, it's not just you and me having dinner tonight."

His eyebrows draw together and he drops his voice. "Please tell me this isn't some bullshit blind date."

I laugh, but the sound can't cover how much I'm freaking out. "No. No way. It's not a blind date. He's here for me."

"Who—"

Dayton chooses this moment to step out from the kitchen into the living room, into Wes's line of sight.

"Hey, Wes."

Wes's green eyes darken, and he looks from Dayton to me and back again, his lip curling into a snarl, face going red, then white. Yes. This is going *very* well. Then he steps into the living room, going toward the source of his rage, and puts himself between me and Day. "I told you to stay away from him." Then he rounds on Day. "I told *you* to stay away from her."

"You knew about this, Wes." I say it as quickly as I can. "You knew he was the father of my baby. Why are you—?"

"Because I still fucking hate it. Looking at you—" He looks like he could spit, and I don't know if he means me or Day. Maybe both. "I've said enough."

Dayton's jaw has gone tense and hard. He shakes his head and steps forward, narrowing the space between them. "You said a lot of things, Wes. Times are different now."

A vein at the side of Wes's neck is bulging. He puts his back to Dayton, which strikes me as a mistake, but he does it anyway. "If you tell me you're living with this guy, I don't know what the fuck I'll do—it's a mistake."

Over Wes's shoulder I see hurt flash through Day's eyes. Then his hard gaze returns.

The right thing to do is to stand up for Day. My boyfriend. The phrase seems ridiculously inadequate, even in my head, for what he means to me. "You know how I feel about you, Wes."

He turns his head and crosses his arms, and I'm struck by how angry his, by how much his anger looks the same as when we were kids. "I trust you. I do. But I've chosen Dayton." I give Day a little nod over Wes's shoulder. His face is grim, but he steps closer and extends his hand. "Please, Wes. This is what's best for everybody."

Wes looks at Day's hand, then up into his eyes.

Then he shakes his head.

My stomach drops. Shit. He's going to walk out and make this hard for everyone. Shit, shit, *shit*.

"Wes—"

Wes puts one hand to his forehead and closes his eyes. Dayton reacts the same way I do, leaning in closer, watching. This is a moment of weakness in the middle of the tension, and my blood surges through my ears at every heartbeat.

Wes drops his hand and looks at me. "It smells good in here. Are you going to show me the kitchen?"

~

DAY AND WES sit down on opposite sides of the table. I feel like a housewife from the 1950s with my plate of garlic bread. All I'm missing is the jaunty apron.

I wish I had an apron.

"Hope you're hungry," Dayton says, his arms folded on the surface of the table. "Sit down, Sunny, I'll get it."

I sit between them and put the plate in the center of the table.

"He's getting the food? Did he cook it?" Wes gets a grip. "Did you *cook*?" He says it just as Day arrives back at the table with a serving plate full of ribs, and another one heaped with homemade potato wedges drowning in butter and seasoning. I will never breathe a word of how hard Day worked on the food. He's normally cavalier in the kitchen. He can *cook*, but he labored over these ribs.

"Summer offered, but I insisted. She's had a rough couple of days."

Wes shoots me a look that's half worry and half irritation. "What happened?"

"Oh...a lot has been going on." The last thing I want to do right now is draw more attention to *everything*.

Dayton brandishes some serving tongs and a spoon and fills everyone's plate, then takes his seat.

"How am I supposed to eat this?" Wes gestures at the plate with both hands. "For all I know, he's trying to poison me."

Day's laughter pops the tension like a balloon. He stands up partway and Wes tenses, hands on the edge of the table, but Day only leans over and plucks a rib and a potato wedge from Wes's plate. He eats the potato wedge first, then bites into the meat. "There, asshole. See? I'm trying to man up here. I'm trying to fucking *make amends.*" Day eats the rest of the meat off the bone and drops it onto his plate, leaving the sauce around his lips. "Don't be a dick."

The corner of Wes's mouth turns upward.

Then he picks up a potato wedge and takes a bite.

I HAVE to stop myself from staring at Dayton.

My chest is a bright center of pride and filled with a love I'm almost embarrassed to be feeling. Not because I love him.

I've always loved him in a puppy love, first crush kind of way. This seems deeper. Truer. He never said a word about how nervous he was about this lunch. He *had* to be nervous, but he never showed it. Part of me wishes he would, but my Day—he tries not to show me anything that'll make my life harder.

I use all of my Heroes on the Homefront skills to keep both of them engaged in small talk—Day, about his new job at Global Connect, and Wes about his Army career.

"Are you happy at Drum, Wes?"

He clears his throat and looks down at his empty plate. "Drum's fine."

I sense that there's more. "But?"

"I'm not sure I'll re-up at the end of my contract."

Dayton's eyebrows rise almost to his hairline. "Had enough?"

"Four deployments? Yeah, that's been enough." He looks at Day across the table. "Not all of them go off without a hitch."

"You're fucking telling *me*."

They lock eyes across the table, and for the first time in my life, my brother backs down. It's an odd sort of blink, and his eyes shift toward the blank wall next to the kitchen. *What was that?* When he resurfaces, attention refocused on his plate, I use the opportunity to complain about how narrow the aisles in the bodega are getting.

The conversations winds its way through safer topics until Wes checks his watch and says he has to head out.

He's the first to stand up from the table.

He looks at me.

He looks at Dayton.

He does not smile.

"Fuck," he says, and my relief is sharp and strong. I see the way his shoulders slump a hairs-breadth when he says it. This is him, accepting the new shape of my life.

We walk him to the door and Day shuts it behind him after he leaves.

I wrap my arms around him and lean in, the weight of his arms around me an anchor for the last of my nerves. "Give him time," I tell him. He rubs one hand down the side of my arm. "He's got a lot to get over before he realizes I'm yours."

"A lot happened before you were mine." There's a burst of pleasure spanning out like a firework in the center of my chest. We're having a *baby* together, and still, hearing him say that—

I pull him closer. "I was *always* yours."

Dayton takes in a sharp breath, and then his lips are on mine, pure and possessive and sweet, and the sound I hear myself making defines sheer pleasure on every level.

Day flips the lock on the door, lifts me up in those arms of his, and carries me to bed.

26

DAYTON

Ten Weeks Later

THE DOOR SWINGS open before I can touch the knob.

"Whoa—"

"*Finally.*"

Summer steps out from behind the door.

She's naked.

I step inside the apartment in a hurry and kick the door shut behind me. "I'm sorry I made you wait."

"Me, too." She rises up on her toes and drops back down again, every inch of her on display, and Jesus, it's a sight. Pregnancy suits her. I could honestly revel in this forever. Ten weeks feels like nothing at all.

To me. Not to her.

It makes me want to relax. To stop looking out for Alexei. I can't do that, but I also can't spend every single moment fretting about him.

I have to enjoy *her*.

At five and a half months, her belly is a perfect curve. I've heard about the *pregnancy glow* before, but Summer is incandescent. Her blonde hair shines, it's even longer than before, and if she let it down, it would brush the top of her pink nipples.

And finally, *finally,* the morning sickness is gone.

In Summer, it's been replaced with hunger. She's hungry all the time, and not just for food.

She wants *me*.

All. The. Time.

I shove down the lingering thought that I am not worthy of this, I'll never be worthy of this, and flip the lock on the front door. Summer smiles rapturously. "I love that sound."

I drink her in while I unbutton my shirt. "How long have you been this way?" She's been perfect forever, and I always knew it, but this takes it to another level.

"What way?" She puts a finger to her lips. "Naked? Waiting for you? Needing you?" Summer takes one step, and then another, toward the bedroom, and taps a finger to her cheek, pretending to think. "I've needed you since that day at the sledding hill." Her smile turns sultry. "Not like this, though. And I've been naked since I got home from work." She kicks at the pile of her clothes near the corner of the couch. Her belly hasn't reached maximum size yet, but she's already avoiding bending down to the floor. I don't care at all.

"Damn that meeting." I drop the shirt and my undershirt to the floor. The pants are the next to go. She's luring me to the bedroom, and I want to be caught.

"Yes, *fuck* that meeting."

"I'd rather fuck you." I'm hard as a rock when I catch up to her at the doorway to the bedroom and run my hands over her breasts—glorious, holy *shit,* they're glorious—over her belly and between her legs. She's already slick. "And you're ready to be fucked."

Summer looks up at me, pink darkening her cheeks, and says the word she knows will start everything. "Please?"

∼

SHE WANTS my hands on her.

Begs for it.

How am I going to say no?

I'm not.

The most comfortable position for pregnant Summer is on her hands and knees on the bed, ass raised up in the air, her glistening pink pussy totally exposed.

It's a miracle I don't come from the sight of it.

"Please, Day, touch me—"

I do.

I touch every inch of her. The small of her back. The curve at the top of her hips. The back of her knees. She loves it when I wrap my hands around her ankles, throws her head back and moans at the pressure there. That's the most startling discovery I've made about Summer. She's not a whips and chains kind of girl, but she likes a little restraint. She likes to feel me holding her down.

Twist my arm.

I release her ankles and climb onto the bed behind her, bending down to speak into her ear while I thread my fingers through the loose bun at the back of her neck and tug. "You need more from me."

She's already panting, and her blue eyes search mine. "I need—"

"Ropes."

Summer's lips drop open and her eyes light up. "You want to tie me up?" I slide one hand back to her ankle and hold her there. She breathes out in a little sigh. "I might want you to tie me up." She bites her lip. "But right now, I want—"

"I know what you want." I bend my head and kiss her at the small of her back, inches away from a place that makes her shiver to brush against. "And to get it, all you need to do…"

"Anything." Her fingers curl around the comforter.

"Hold very, *very* still."

Summer grips the headboard, up on her knees. It's a fantastic rhythm, my cock buried deep in her sweet, sweet pussy every stroke, her hips rocking back against me. She wants me all the way inside of her.

She likes to be *fucked*.

If I ever thought about her this way before, I imagined that she'd like it gentle. Slow. Soft.

And she does, about once every month.

Today is not one of those days.

She spreads her legs wider, giving me more room, and presses back harder against me. I can feel her tightening against me. I can feel her on the edge, and I know just what she likes.

On the next stroke, I pin her by the hips. I'm so deep inside that every move she makes is a wonderful torture. Then I pull her back from the headboard against my chest, drawing one arm up, and then the other, so her breasts rise as her arms settle around my neck.

"You—" She struggles for words. "You—"

"It's time for *you* to come."

"Pinned down like this?" Her voice is low, pleading.

"Pinned down like this, my cock buried inside you. You can't get away." She trembles against me, and I circle one nipple with the pad of my fingers, then drag them all the way down her body to her clit.

Summer arcs upward with a little cry, but I hold her against me. She's so close. *So* close.

The slightest pressure on her clit starts the rolling thunder of her release, and she bucks against my arms, against my hands. It doesn't matter. I am stronger, and I am relentless, and her arms go tight around my neck as she comes. I get

my hand to her mouth just in time to catch a howl of pleasure that's almost a scream. Her muscles are wound so tight
around me that she very nearly takes me with her.

But instead...

Instead, when the orgasm subsides, she uncurls my arm
from her chest and crawls forward.

I'm still inside her when she arches her back, sticking her
ass in the air, and says, "More."

SUMMER WATCHES me as I sprawl back against the pillows.
She's pulled her hair into a slightly less disheveled bun on
the top of her head and lays on her side.

I close my eyes.

"I like seeing you this way." She puts the back of her hand
against my cheek and runs it down to my chin, resting it on
my chest.

"What way?"

"Basking."

Through the warmth of the afterglow, a pain yawns at the
end of my stump. The sheet against the skin wasn't an issue
until now—against a raw spot? I don't know—and the
burning travels down through the foot that isn't there,
causing non-existent toes to curl into a cramp. I try to keep
my face neutral. Summer sees the struggle.

"Are you going to your appointments?"

"Yes."

"Liar."

"Most of them."

"When's the next one?"

"Next week." I open my eyes and bask again in the concern on her face. "Next week I have a fitting for the new prosthesis."

Her mouth drops into a round O. "Already? That came up *fast*."

I think about the years I've spent with this shitty temporary one, and close my eyes again. All those steps I took. Why did I *wait* so long? Why did I wait so long to be a decent fucking human? I could have started that process a long time ago, after what happened. It's better this way. I'm doing work that actually matters. I have Summer, who is ravenous for me in a way I never could have predicted. Never. "Not nearly fast enough."

She sighs happily. "One week and you'll have your new leg. I'm so excited for you."

"Me, too."

"Although—" There's a wicked tone in her voice that makes me open my eyes again. Summer grins, a glint in those blues I'd recognize anywhere. I'm hard. Instantly. "When it comes to legs, you have an average of two..." She takes my cock in her hand and squeezes.

"You want more already?"

She bites her lip. "I *need* more."

"Jesus."

"Pregnancy makes me horny," she says with a pout. "I can't help it."

"I know it," I tell her, and put my hands on her waist. Pregnant or not, she's nothing to lift, to bring down on top of me. "I love it."

She lifts her hips up and angles herself over me, already wet and wanting. "Please? Can I?" Her smile is like a queen's. The question is only a formality. No—a game. A sexy, teasing game that I'll never get enough of as long as I live.

"I'm all yours." I tighten my grip on her hips. "Ride away."

Four Weeks Later

THE BABY DOES a spin move and kicks out *hard* into the front of my belly. It catches me off guard right by Carla's desk.

There is no such thing as *breezing in to work* anymore. Not at six and a half months pregnant. Not in August in the city. I'm wearing flip flops shamelessly, and my entire wardrobe consists of skirts and sleeveless maternity tanks.

"You're starting to waddle, sweetheart," she says, grinning up at me from her ergonomic chair.

"I think this baby's walking already." She laughs, and the sound follows me down the hall to my office.

God, I'm happy.

I'm so happy, it's like breathing in Florida air every second—that warm, content feeling you get when you step inside the gates at the Magic Kingdom. I'd say that Day is like my own personal Magic Kingdom, but even thinking it borders on ridiculously sappy.

He does things nobody's ever done for me before.

Not that I've been pregnant, up until this point in my life.

Still, none of the men I had short-lived flings with in college ever cared for me this way. I never cared for them either, but it's so different with Day. Like the hotel he took me to after I got out of the hospital. We spent the night at the Knickerbocker overlooking Times Square and watched the tourists going in and out. There was room service. There was a bubble bath.

There was Dayton.

Carla appears in the doorway of my office. "Messages," she says, and drops a little pile of notes on my desk. The baby flips over.

"I know," I say. "Let's hope not all of them want callbacks."

It's not that I don't want to do my job. It's that long-winded phone conversations are starting to take my breath away— literally. When I'm sitting down, the baby presses up against my lungs, and the more I talk, the harder it is to catch my breath. I can alleviate it by standing up, but try *standing* for the length of a phone call. It's a duel between my feet and my back, and my feet usually give out first.

I start in on the calls, pressing the phone between my neck and my shoulder, and tap my fingers against the surface of my desk.

My left hand looks totally naked.

I'm pregnant enough for people to notice.

I'm not ashamed that this is Dayton's baby.

I listen to the first veteran's answering machine pick up.

We should get married.

Beep.

"We should—" Oh, God. Heat rushes to my cheeks, both at the egregious mistake I *almost* made and the thought of standing anywhere with Dayton in a white dress. "Hi, this is Summer Sullivan from Heroes on the Homefront. I'm calling because you had emailed us some preliminary information, and I wanted to follow up with you on the services we offer. Give me a call back when you can." I rattle off my number and hang up.

Then I dig my cell phone out of my purse.

The idea that flashes through my mind just now? It calls for an emergency lunch with Whitney.

"YOU LOOK *SO GOOOOOOOOOOOOOOOD*!!"

Whitney's shriek stops traffic in the trendy little restaurant she insisted on meeting at for lunch. She doesn't care at all. She throws her arms around me and squeezes. The hostess stifles a smile and looks away.

"Dying. Air." I choke the words out and Whit releases me from her death grip. Then she pushes me back so she can get another look at me.

"You are the cutest pregnant person on the *planet*," she

squeals, and claps her hands. "Are you hungry? You must be hungry. I'm starving to death, so you must be dead."

"I'm actually dead," I tell her, because it's partially true. I've been hungry since I texted her at nine-fifteen, and that's *with* the doughnuts Hazel brought in.

Whit links her arm through mine and turns to the hostess. "Your finest table for my very best friend."

We're seated with water and a basket of bread—thank God —when she levels the *tell me now* gaze at me. "Spill it."

I blush and rub my thumb around the empty space on my ring finger. "It's stupid."

She rolls her eyes. "You texted me about an *emergency lunch*. There's no time to waste. What's on your mind?" Whit leans back and sighs. "God, this was easier when we lived together."

"It was." I'm a little wistful for my apartment with Whit, mainly because of her bright, shining personality—no joke —but the thought of coming home to Dayton every day makes my heart sing. "I miss it."

Which is why I want to run this by her.

She gives me a sidelong look. "You don't miss it *that* much. Are you kidding me? Dayton is *hot*." Whit fans herself with the wine list. "That body..."

That body makes me blush all over again. "That's why I wanted to talk to you."

"Because of his *body*?" Whitney clasps her hands in front of her and closes her eyes. "Tell me this is a picture emergency. An emergency wherein...you have pictures to show me."

"Oh my *God*. I do not have *pictures* to show you. This is—" I cover my face in my hands. "This is serious, Whit."

Her palms slap against the table. "How serious?"

"*Really* serious."

"Okay." I can't see her, but I know she's rearranging her expression into her serious face. "I'm listening."

I take a deep breath and uncover my face. "I want to marry him."

Whitney considers me, her eyes narrowing. "I'm going to stop you there."

"Whit—"

"Waiter. Waiter!" She doesn't snap her fingers, thank God, but the waiter hustles back over nonetheless. "Two virgin daiquiris. Fast as you can."

～

IT TASTES SO good that I double-check with the waiter to be absolutely sure there's no alcohol in it.

He assures me there's not, his eyes flickering down to the curve of my belly.

"Exactly," Whitney says. "I don't know why she's worried. All the drinking she's done before this—"

"I have *not* done any drinking. Thank you for checking on the drink."

The waiter grins and leaves.

We both sip our daiquiris.

"So you want to marry him."

"Yes, but it's—it's more than that." The daiquiri is a good substitute for real food for the moment. I want my hamburger to arrive at the table so much that I feel like pounding the handle of my steak knife into the wood and letting out a primal scream, but I don't, because I am civilized. "We haven't had...you know, a traditional relationship. So I thought maybe we could have a non-traditional proposal."

Whitney grabs another piece of bread from the basket. "Like...you want him to take you somewhere super mundane instead of to a fancy restaurant?"

"No. I want to propose to *him*."

"Oh. *Oh!*" Whitney's eyes go left, then right, wide and excited. "You *have* to. That would be absolutely perfect."

"You think so?"

Her expression softens. "Sunny, I've never seen you this happy."

Because she is my best friend in the world, I can say to her the secret fear that's been prickling at the back of my mind in the moments I wake up at night and listen to the sound of Day's breathing, slow and deep. "What if it's just hormones?" I take another piece of bread and bite into it, anything to keep the impending mood swing at bay. "They say your hormones can make you turn more into the dad. He's not—he's not a teenager anymore. He's been through shit. What if that all—"

"That's *nonsense*." Whitney is deadly serious. "You've been in love with that guy since you were a kid. You couldn't stop yourself from talking about him even before he showed up."

"He's different now."

"Is he?" Whitney leans back to let the waiter put her plate down in front of her, and I do the same on my side of the table. "Isn't this the guy who ran down a hill after you in the snow? Isn't this the guy who danced with you when you got stood up, and never said a word about the fact that you were *just a kid*?"

"Yes, but—"

"He bought you morning sickness shit off the Internet."

What happened *after* one of those lollipops makes me shiver, an echo of the delight.

"Whit, there are things he's done—things he's seen—that he won't tell me about."

She cuts into her salad, the knife splitting the lettuce with a crisp crunch. "All men have secrets. But he's more than a man. He's *yours*."

I can't argue with that.

≈

ON THE WAY back to the office, I stop at a streetlight. There's only one other person I need to consult with about this ridiculous proposal idea.

Baby stretches, pressing against both sides of my belly at once.

"Should I propose to Daddy?" I look around to make sure

nobody catches me talking to myself. "One kick, yes. Two kicks, no."

There's a pause.

I didn't count on *zero* kicks.

Then I feel it: a single, solid *thud*, directly to my spine.

28

Four Weeks Later

SUMMER PULLS OPEN the door to the jewelry store with such overly exaggerated confidence that I wonder if she's faking it, but once we're inside, she inhales a deep breath and her shoulders relax.

I put one of my hands on her shoulder and slide my hand down her arm. It's meant to seem casually affectionate, but even now, my breath hitches from the wonderment of touching her.

It sounds cheesy, but it's the truth.

"What are you looking for?" If jewelry is what she wants, jewelry is what she'll get. I've never known her to be much into jewelry, but pregnancy has made her more spontaneous. Who knows? I didn't fight her when she wanted to come to Williamsburg instead of staying in bed all weekend.

The lighting in the jewelry store is fucking fantastic, and it makes her look regal, even in her drab gray yoga leggings and a pink-colored pregnancy top that makes her belly the center of attention. Not that she can help it. She's gorgeous and blonde and has the kind of perfectly round swell that could be on the front of the motherhood magazines they have all over at her OB's office.

A blush matching the shade of her shirt spreads across her cheeks. "I want to see their selection."

"Look—your wish came true." I wave my hand in the direction of the display cases, and she laughs, her shoulders rising and falling against my arm. "Where should we start?"

"On one side, I guess." Summer waddles over to the first display case on the left and peers inside for exactly one second before she moves on. She does the same with the next one, and then with the third.

I follow along behind her. I don't know what she's looking for, but a lot of the pieces behind the glass are delicate and shiny. Each and every one of them would look good on her.

Four cases. Five. No, no, no.

I catch her by the elbow, which is more of a kind gesture than a necessity. She can't go anywhere fast—not this pregnant. "I want in on this," I tell her, and she bites her lip. "Can we...narrow it down by the *kind* of jewelry?" We both look into the sixth case together. "Are you looking for the perfect necklace? A bracelet? That one's nice." I point to one with blue stones that would bring out the color of her eyes. Her eyes linger over a delicate gold band with a sapphire that is edged by two tiny diamonds.

"No. None of those." Summer takes in a deep breath and steps over to a wide case along the back wall.

We both look down into the case together, and I put my hand on the back of her neck. Her hair is swept up in a loose bun at the back of her head. It's my favorite style, because when I place my palm in this position, it makes all the tension in her body melt away.

"This is men's jewelry."

Summer turns and looks me in the eye. "I know."

"Rings...."

"I know."

"They're mainly wedding bands."

She's solemn as fuck. "I know."

Our eyes catch then, her face lit up from the glow of the jewelry case.

"What's happening right now?"

Summer looks toward the ceiling, blushing a deep red. "Just —look at the rings with me. Okay?" There's a heavy pause. "Do you see any that you like?"

We turn back to look in the case. There are rows of bands. Some of them are so ornate that they look like some shit that crazy King Henry would have worn. I can't see myself wearing any of those.

Summer stands quietly, swaying side to side in the way that she always does now, and it creeps up on me again.

It starts as a pain in my non-existent left foot, like a pebble wedged under my big toe, and it starts creeping up to my stump. I shift my weight on the prosthetic. It doesn't help. It twists its way up into my lower back and taps at the base of my neck. *You're going to be her biggest mistake.* The waves of tension fold and unfold, taking up more room in my gut. *You're less than a man, but you're still a threat.*

I rub one hand over my face, swiping away at the dark thoughts. Summer doesn't know that I'm kept lying awake most nights into the early hours, watching the street for any sign of Alexei. She doesn't know that I've searched and searched for other apartments—even similar jobs for her— in other cities, just so we can get away. I can't tell her that Wes was right about me. That I turned out this way despite the Army—despite everything.

I especially can't tell her that now.

"Day?" She threads her fingers through mine. For a moment, it feels like I'm on solid ground. "If you don't like any of them, it's okay."

Her eyes are filled with a wistful blend of hope and fear that I intuitively recognize at my very core. She so badly wants to do what's right. She is hoping this is it, but she must fear that she's pushed me in the wrong direction.

Focus.

I look back down into the case and squeeze her hand.

Then I see it.

It's down at the end of the third row, the very last spot. Thin. Gold. No embellishments.

"That one."

The jeweler treads up to the case and lifts the band I pointed to out of the case so we can see it. Summer's entire face lights up when I slip it onto my finger.

It's a perfect fit.

She doesn't hesitate. "We'll take it."

At the register, once the wedding band has been tucked inside in a small black velvet box and placed carefully in one of the store's trademark silver paper bags, we have a brief difference of opinion over who's going to pay. Summer uses her pregnant belly to box me out at the counter and shoves her credit card into the man's hand, even as I try to get mine to him first.

"Pregnant lady wins," she announces victoriously, and it makes me laugh. The pain at the base of my neck eases.

She accepts the bag from the salesperson and waddles alongside me as we head out onto the sidewalk, a sultry and damp wall of air hitting us as we open the door. Summer's eyes are luminous in the afternoon sunlight. Before I can step to the curb, she curls her hand through the crook of my elbow. "I want this," she says.

She doesn't elaborate.

"Are you proposing?"

Her face turns a deep scarlet. "Not *yet*."

"Good. I want a turn, too."

Summer tilts her face up toward mine. Her lips are soft and yielding against mine when they meet, and someone down the block whistles. She doesn't pull away at the sound. Instead, she leans in.

When she pulls back from the kiss, we're both superheated. Her hand goes to her lips, but her gaze settles on something far away. "Can I ask you something?"

"Anything."

"I hate asking this."

"Do it anyway."

"Could you—" Summer holds the little paper back from the jewelry shop to her chest. "Could you try and make up with Wes?"

"Make up with *Wes*? I made him ribs. If that's not enough, then—"

"I'm *serious*. I know he was an asshole. But I don't want things to be tense when the baby gets here. I feel like there's something he's not telling me, and I don't want—I just don't want—"

I smooth a hand over her hair. "Sunny."

"Yeah?"

"I'll make up and be friends with him, if that's what you want. I'm not going to come between you and your brother." I put two fingers under her chin and lift her face to mine. "I'll even make him ribs *again,* if that's what it takes."

I kiss her a second time. Summer murmurs into my mouth, and every muscle in my body wants to leap for the curb. Get this woman into a *cab*. Get her into my *bed*.

She laughs as I twist away from her. "I never thought we'd—"

There's a crash and then a *screech*, metal on metal, and I jump back on instinct, shielding her with my arms. What the fuck. What the *fuck*?

It's a car, screaming up toward us onto the sidewalk. He

clipped one of the protective iron fences bordering some flowers at the edge of the street.

I hustle Summer backward, adrenaline masking the pain in my leg, but the vehicle's engine revs. The car reverses, then lurches forward *again*. The iron fence bends, breaks, and the vehicle's driver is accelerating, that fucker is *accelerating* toward us. The back wheels catch the curb, but the front end of the car brushes against my pant leg. Holy fuck. If I had a real leg, he'd have clipped it. Crushed it. I don't know.

"Hey!" A man is running toward us from the next corner, and a shop owner hustles out after him. The street is chaos, horns honking, taxi drivers screaming at the car, and at the center of it, Summer gasps. The car lurches forward another inch, but he doesn't quite clear the curb.

The driver is close enough for me to see him.

Alexei.

Eyes wild, hands braced on the steering wheel, mouth stretched open wide. Is he laughing or shouting? I have no idea, but his eyes meet mine and his expression contorts into a sneer. It's one of pure rage, ugly and unrestrained.

He rolls down the window and his voice spills out onto the street. It's a long slur of curse words and something unintelligible.

"Move. *Move.*" I lock my arm around Summer and back her up into the doorway of the jewelry store. "Open the door. Open the door."

I can't see her, but I hear when she finally gets the latch open. "Oh, my God, Day, oh, my God—"

"Go in!"

I feel her step away from me, into the store, and brace both of my hands against the recessed entryway. He's not going to get to her. Not now. Not ever.

He rolls the window back up.

Inside the car, Alexei turns his head to the right and then to left. People are reacting—fucking rare for New York City— and the man from the opposite corner is at his windshield, both hands up, tapping on the hood. "What are you thinking, man? Are you having a stroke?" He shouts the words at the windshield, but Alexei is looking at me.

I don't flinch.

Fuck. His mouth makes the shape of the curse and then his shoulders go down. The car reverses back out into traffic and a cab swerves to miss him.

With a screech of tires, he disappears into the line of cars. I follow him as long as I can. I follow that car until he's out of sight.

All I can hear is my own heartbeat.

All I can feel is sickness rising in my throat.

I'm bringing this onto her. Me. It's all me. It's all my fault.

I can't do it.

29

SUMMER

THE POWER DRILL hums in Dayton's hand. He's installing an extra deadbolt on the front door of our apartment.

The silver bag from the jewelry store sits abandoned on the tiny kitchen island. I can't decide whether I should be sitting or standing. If someone bursts through the door, even with the deadbolt in place, I want to be on my feet and ready to run

The last screw goes in tight. Dayton shoves every lock home, then tests the door with his hand, pulling on it with his full weight. The door doesn't budge. My heart beats high in my throat. Part of that is the baby's fault, but mostly it's because of the guy in the car. He tried to *kill* us. My heart's been racing ever since it happened. The cab ride home wasn't even enough to calm me down. Not that it was a relaxing cab ride—Dayton made us switch cars three times over the course of the ten-mile ride.

Dayton drops his tools onto the table in the entryway. As soon as they hit the wooden surface he turns and rushes past my spot in the living room. He hobbles into the bedroom. His foot must be killing him. What the hell does he need in the bedroom?

I remain where I've been stationed, watching him install the lock. I take a series of calming breaths, steadying myself, before taking one last deep breath and straightening my posture. This is fine.

Yes, it was scary when the car jumped the curb and tried to *kill us,* but I can't freak out anymore. Not anymore. The baby senses everything that I feel.

I put my hands on my belly and baby rolls beneath my touch, a languid turn, as if nothing is wrong in the world.

"You're right," I murmur. "There's nothing to worry about. I'll keep you safe." Goosebumps rise up on the back of my arms. I haven't said it before, but future me will say it countless times. It's a blow to the heart, isn't it? You meant those words as a promise, but nothing's a guarantee.

I follow Dayton into the bedroom. He's rummaging through the dresser drawers, one by one, methodically searching beneath my panties, beneath his shirts, beneath the spare sheet sets I can't bend down to reach any more.

"Day."

He straightens up and turns his head to look at me, and I'm struck by his expression, a combination of determination and terror.

"Come here?" I hold my arms out to him and he limps across the room, the intensity of each step showing in his face, and then he bends all six-feet, three inches of him to wrap me firmly in his embrace.

We stand that way until my heart isn't racing anymore.

"I have to go."

I must have misheard him, with my ear pressed up against his chest like that. "What?"

Dayton holds me at arm's length then, his dark eyes burdened with pain. "I can't stay here with you, Sunny." He lets me go and runs both hands through his hair. His voice hitches. "He's after me."

"Who's *he*?" He turns away from me, but I stop him, gripping his elbow and drawing his attention back to my eyes. "No. You need to tell me what's going on."

"It's nothing you need to know about. It's nothing you *should* know about. The less you know—"

My pulse pounds in my ears. "The less I know, the more fucking terrified I am, Day." My palms are sweating and I feel like I've stopped breathing. He steps back over to the dresser and begins rifling through it again. "What are you *looking* for?"

He straightens up, blows a breath out between his lips. "A *gun*, Summer. I'm looking for a gun. But I don't have one." Day's jaw works. "I don't have one, because where was I going to keep one while I was living in that shithole of an apartment? I couldn't trust any of them with a gun, much less myself—" He roughly shakes his head as if to erase what he was thinking. This is more than he meant to say.

"Dayton, you can't do this. You can't walk away from me because you *think* you're dangerous."

He lets out a short, sharp laugh. "I *am* dangerous. I've told you that before. I warned you about my past. It's back. Don't you get that? What else has to happen for you to understand?"

"Yes." My voice trembles, but I force myself to hold my head up high. "I work with people who've had rough lives, Day, and I'm not a little girl."

"I'm sorry." Day steels himself and heads into the walk-in closet, emerging a couple of seconds later with a black duffel bag. "I'm sorry, Summer. I know you're not a kid. But you have no idea—" He closes his eyes and curses under his breath. "You have no idea what it was like when I came back home. You have no idea what people like him are capable of."

"I was standing on the sidewalk right next to you."

A flash of emotion streaks across Day's face, and he's at my side again. "Did you see the man in the car? Did you see his face?"

I search my memory and can picture the man's profile, his pale face planted behind the windshield, his nasally voice drilling into me from inside the car. "Yes, but—"

"Have you ever seen him before?" Day braces his hands on my arms, holding me still. "Summer, it's fucking important! Have you seen him before?"

"*No*." Something is tingling at the back of my mind. "The only thing was—"

"Tell me. Right now."

"I'm *trying*." I take a deep breath to concentrate. "The only thing was that his voice sounded familiar." Where have I heard that voice before? "I think he was the one who followed me that day." *That day* is code for the last time I ran outside alone.

Day's face hardens and turns pale. He releases me and returns to retrieve his duffel bag that fell to the floor when I mentioned standing next to him on the street. It takes him all of five seconds to yank open his dresser drawer, yank out an armful of clothes, and shove them into the bag, but in those five seconds, my mind struggles to process a memory.

"That's not the only time I've heard that voice," I say, thinking out loud, and I tap my fingers in the air, just like I do when I'm sitting at my desk at Heroes on the Homefront.

Just like I do on my desk.

"He called my office once," I recall, the words floating reflectively into the air as the memory dawns on me, and Dayton freezes in place from his packing. "He left a message that included my name, then there was the sound of some weird breathing. It was when I was at home. They forwarded the message from my office to my phone."

Day drops the bag. "You're done there."

"What?" I say, incredulous.

"You're done working there. Call in and tell them you're done." He snatches his phone off the top of the dresser and tries to press it into my hands.

"Dayton, no. I'm not quitting my job because—"

"He tried to terrorize me...by using *you*." Day's voice is deadly serious. "He followed you in his car. He almost *killed us* today, and all for the kind of revenge that's never going to

—" He closes his eyes, swallows hard. "I don't care if you call in or not. You're not going back there, and that's final."

The injustice of this, coupled with the adrenaline from the episode on the sidewalk and the ache at seeing his consuming fear, makes my throat tighten. "Oh, yeah? Is that what you think?" Who does he think he is? My *dad*? My *brother*? Does everyone in my entire life think I'm too stupid to make my own decisions?

Dayton levels his gaze at me. "Yes."

The first tear slips down my cheek, but I'll be damned if I cry any harder than that. "You're wrong." My voice trembles. I hate it for trembling. "I'm going back to work on Monday, like I always do. My clients need me."

"They'll get by."

"Will they?" I advance on Dayton, every step looking more ridiculous than the last, I'm sure. "Where would *you* be right now if it wasn't for me? Killing yourself at that factory, that's where. The rest of my clients deserve the same help *you* got.*"

"I didn't *want* your help," Dayton roars, blood rushing to his cheeks. "I didn't want *anyone's* fucking help. I only went because that asshole at the VA insisted. If I wanted to quit crushing the fuck out of my leg, he said I had to—" His fists clench at his sides in an attempt to rein in his anger. "I didn't want *anyone's* help. I didn't *deserve* anyone's help. And if that's what this is about—"

"That's *not* what this is about," I shout back at him, fear and rage and hope all coalescing together in my chest. "This is about the fact that *I love you*. And I'm pregnant with your fucking baby. And if you walk out on me right now, with that guy lurking out there, then—then—" It leaves me breathless, gasping, and now the tears gush forth, the dam bursting. "How would that be the right thing to do, you asshole? How could you *say* that to me? How could you threaten me with that? You're worse than *him*."

I turn away quickly to hide my emotions, heading blindly for the bathroom. I lean over the sink and turn on the cold water, the rushing sound comforting.

A minute later I sense Dayton standing behind me. He says something I don't hear, and then I hear, "Sunny."

His hand comes down on my shoulder, tentative, apologetic, but I'm still fucking furious. I shrug it off. "Don't touch me." The water is louder than my own voice. "Don't touch me. Just *don't* touch me."

30

S<small>UMMER IS</small> silent as we walk down the hallway to the ultrasound room.

She's spoken to me twice today. The first time was to say *my ultrasound is at twelve-thirty.* The second time was to say *you don't need to be there.*

Fuck *that*. I'm going to be here, even if she's freezing me out.

I was awake when she started crying again last night, soundlessly, her shoulders shaking under the comforter, but when I tried to take her into my arms, she went stiff and still and refused to let me touch her.

I feel like shit.

I feel like shit on every level, from the worn-away liner in my prosthetic to the sleepless grit in my eyes to the fact that even when I'm trying to get as far away from my past as I can, it always catches up with me. No fucking surprise. I'm a man without both of his feet.

It was only one day.

The rest of it—the rest of it, I've lost track of. A few weeks? A few months? I was swimming in a sea of pain, endless and excruciating, and I knew it was my punishment for that lapse in my attention on that mountain. I wasn't in the right frame of mind when I made the choice. I'd explain it to Summer now that the desperate need for flight has passed and I've settled into the fact that we're staying where we are, but she will not speak to me. She won't even look at me. She came to this appointment in a separate cab.

She lies back on the table and pulls up her shirt, her belly big but still perfect, her skin creamy and beautiful. The ultrasound tech makes small talk. It all washes over me, meaningless and generic. *It's hot out there, huh? You must be miserable. No, it's all worth it in the end. With my two...*

Summer's face is lit up by the ultrasound machine, and I can see from here that she's exhausted. Heavy, dark bags under her eyes. Her mouth in a thin line. My heart wrenches. This should be a joyful experience for her, or as much as it can be. Hot, sickening spasms of guilt sear across my gut. It would be a beautiful experience, if it wasn't for me.

"Here's baby's head," the tech says, and presses the wand into Summer's belly so we can both see. The profile is perfect. I don't linger on the screen.

Summer's face softens. "Beautiful," she whispers. I want so badly to be holding her hand.

"Did you find out the sex at your twenty-week appointment?" The tech's voice is carefully neutral. She's not going to push us one way or the other. There's zero pressure in the room as she swipes the wand around, checking the heart, the lungs, the fingers and toes.

"No," Summer says, and the longing in her voice takes me aback. We'd laughed at the twenty-week appointment. It was going to be a grand surprise, whether the baby was a boy or a girl, but even in the dark, I can see fresh tears pooling at the corners of Summer's eyes.

I clear my throat. "Could we find out today?"

She looks at me for the first time since last night. "Is that what you want?"

I scoot closer on the rolling stool and put my hand on the edge of the bed. Not touching her, but available. "What I want is for you to know that some things aren't surprises. There are things you can count on."

Her chin quivers. "Like what?"

I take her hand in mine and lift her knuckles to my lips. "Me."

Summer blinks, once, then twice. "Are you sure about that?" She doesn't add the rest. She doesn't add *because last night you scared me so badly I cried myself to sleep.*

"I've never been more sure of anything in my life."

"Call it, Dad," interjects the ultrasound tech. "Do you want to know if baby is a boy or a girl?"

"We do."

The tech gives us an encouraging nod, her dark hair shining in the light of the screen, and sweeps the wand confidently around. There is our baby, suspended in Summer's belly, small and perfect and—

"There she is. It's a girl!" The tech says it without warning, and Summer gives a little *whoop*. I feel her joy straight through her hand. Even if I couldn't see her smile, I'd feel it in every cell of my body.

"A girl," I echo. There's a burst of light and warmth at the center of my chest dawns like a sunrise. A little girl. I can see her lying in Summer's arms. I can see her cooing in mine. My two girls. The sunrise turns to a hard light.

I'll do whatever it takes to protect them.

Even if that means going toe-to-toe with Alexei.

Even if that means atoning for what I've done.

But the future seems far away as the ultrasound tech helps Summer wipe the gel from her skin before she heads down the hall to print off pictures for us to take with us. This time, the prints will say BABY GIRL SULLIVAN on them.

As soon as the door shuts behind her, I fold Summer into my arms. She leans into me as far as she can, bending her head to rest it on my shoulder. "I'm not going to cry."

"Don't cry," I say into her ear. "We're having a little girl."

"*Your* little girl," she says, and pushes back to look at me. "Don't—" Summer swallows and lifts her chin. "Please don't ever—"

"I'll never say that to you again." I put my thumb on the ridge of her chin. "I'll never leave you again." I mean those words with everything in my soul.

I mean it, but in the back of my mind is the gnawing truth: I might not be able to control it.

But that's far from this room and this moment. "You made

me so *angry*," Summer breathes, and then she laughs out loud, wiping tears from her eyes. "We have a lot to talk about."

"Let's celebrate first. I want to take my girls out for lunch."

"*Yes.* Let's invite Whitney." Summer realizes what I meant a beat later. "And…the baby can come along, too."

The shape of the words feels right in my mouth. "But Sunny?"

"Yeah?"

"Promise me—" Now *I'm* getting choked up, and there's no way I'm going to put on that kind of show in front of the ultrasound tech. She *would* walk back into the room during just that kind of moment. "Just promise me you'll be safe. I can't lose both of you."

"Lose us?" She laughs, but then her face transforms into a serious expression. "Day, the only way you're going to lose us is if *you* walk away." It takes my breath away. But then Summer grins. "I don't know how far you'd get on one foot, but I wouldn't recommend trying it."

"You are *unbelievable.*" I laugh out loud, the tension falling away from my shoulders, and wrap her up in a bear hug.

"Baby. Baby," she says, pushing back playfully. "Leave room for the baby."

"Is this enough room?" I bend and kiss her, and she opens her pretty lips for me just as the ultrasound tech opens the door.

31

"WHAT WE'RE all going to do—even you, Linda—Linda, eyes up here!" My mom, along with everyone else attending my baby shower, laughs at Whitney's performance, the room filling with the happy sound. "We're all going to guess how big Summer's belly is." Whitney looks over in my direction and raises one eyebrow. "I know. She's in love with this idea."

Seated behind Whit in the place of honor, my belly on prominent display in a pink maternity sundress, I roll my eyes at her announcement.

"I have already taken the measurement, so this won't be embarrassing for Summer—" More laughter follows. "The guest with the closest guess wins a gift card to Sephora. If you're a nice person, you'll take this lovely pregnant woman with you."

Whitney totally transformed the idea of my baby shower from a yellow celebration of gender-neutral everything to a pink explosion, and she did it inside of a week. I'd be impressed if I didn't feel *so* pregnant, and I still have six weeks to go.

Six long weeks.

Another Braxton Hicks contraction squeezes at my belly, tightening down over baby girl. Baby Girl Sullivan, reads the name on her ultrasound pictures. Baby Girl Sullivan. That's all fine and good, but I want her to have Dayton's last name.

I want to have Dayton's last name.

As for first names...

More and more these days, I feel my mind slipping into daydreams. It's getting harder to sleep, what with the extra weight on my torso and the heartburn, so whenever my mind wanders during the day, the images come. Holding the baby in my arms. Whispering to her. Calling her... what? What am I calling her?

I didn't have a name picked out when I first learned I was pregnant, and I still don't have a short list.

What if it doesn't turn out?

The doubt whispers the warning at the back of my mind and I shiver. The A/C is barely turned up high enough to keep me cool in my current state, but the sun on my back feels hot. I can't win.

What if it *doesn't,* though? The fight with Day earlier this week shook me to my core. Things seemed okay after the ultrasound, but when we were outside, back in the light of day, I saw a stiffness, a tension, that hasn't gone away. He's thinking about something, and he won't tell me what it is.

It sets me on edge.

A cheer goes up, and I realize the game is over. One of my college friends, Mindy, has won the gift certificate, and she comes to the front of the room and throws her arms around my neck, promising to take me to Sephora anytime I'd like.

"No need," I tell her. "Enjoy it for yourself." The thought of standing in Sephora—or standing anywhere, for that matter —for long enough to make a purchase makes my entire soul feel fatigued.

After the games, there's a round of picture-taking. Each of the shower guests swirl around me in different combinations, placing their hands on my pregnant belly. They're tender about it, and despite the fact that I do *not* want to stand for any longer than necessary, it fills me with a kind of sisterly glow.

My mom is last in line.

"I don't know if she's excited," I told Whitney on the phone last weekend. The two of them planned the shower together at a reception hall outside the city. "She never liked Dayton's family." She never seemed to dislike Dayton, but I was a kid. What the hell do I know?

"Sunny, stop. She's thrilled. It's her first grandbaby! She wouldn't care if this baby was the product of a steamy one-night stand."

"In a way..."

"Ha. If that was a one-night stand, then I'm in a *lot* of happy relationships right now."

We're happy. *We're happy*. I repeat the words to myself over and over again. I can ignore that this current state of happiness is a temporary peace treaty. I can feel Day drawing part of himself away from me, even now. And he's not here.

"Oh, baby girl," my mom says softly, asking me permission with her eyes to touch my belly. I nod to her, and she puts both hands against the swell under my dress. "Oh! That was a *kick*!"

"She's strong." My mom beams, then turns me gently toward the photographer.

"A picture with my girl."

The camera clicks. "Ugh. This angle is terrible, Mom. Take another one so I don't look like a beached whale."

"Only temporary, daughter mine. And you don't look like a beached whale. You look beautiful."

Whitney stands behind the photographer, inviting everyone to eat. My mom kisses me on the temple and moves to return to her role as co-hostess. I grab her hand at the last second.

She turns, worry creasing her forehead. "Is everything okay?"

"Yes. I mean, my feet hurt, but—" I laugh nervously, then turn her away from the guests, our backs making a protective shield, the baby wedged between us. "Mom." I'm suddenly desperate for her approval. It's stupid. It's too late to change anything now, even if I wanted to, which I don't. "Are you okay with this?"

She glances over our shoulders. "The party's beautiful,

Sunny. Everyone's having a great time. Why? Did someone say something?"

"No, not—not the party. *This.*" I put my hand on my belly. "With Dayton."

I've been afraid to say his name, to invoke any judgment. I don't want that. Not today.

"Summer."

I look up into my mom's eyes. Blue, just like mine.

Her expression has never been more serious.

"If you're not happy," she says slowly. "If he's done *anything* to—"

I clutch her arm. "No. *No.* That's not what I'm saying. I—" I shake my head, the words disappearing even as I try to say them. "I'm in love with him." My heart beats hard against my rib cage. "But I don't want to spend my life in a shadow."

"What shadow?"

"If you—" I'm struggling for breath now, I'm so nervous. "If you hate him. If you hate that kind of person. I don't want to ruin everything for you if that's what—"

My mom faces me, taking my hands in hers. "Sunny, take a breath."

I do.

"I've known Dayton almost as long as I've known Wes." Her mouth curves upward into a fond smile. "He hasn't always been on the straight and narrow, but what teenage boy doesn't make mistakes?"

"Everybody makes mistakes."

Her eyes stay on mine, searching. "You're an adult. If Dayton makes you happy, then I'm happy *for* you." She shakes her head a little. "Those tattoos, though—" She saw them for the first time last night, when my parents took us out to dinner. It's the first time they've been to the city since we moved in together. Both of them still work, so it's not as if they've been avoiding it, but— "Those tattoos are something else."

"I like them," I tell her, and I honestly do. Tracing my fingers down the lines of them after sex is one of my favorite things.

"That's all that matters." She lets go of my hands and pulls me in for a hug. "Seriously, Summer, are you getting cold feet about moving in with him?"

I laugh out loud. "The last thing I have is cold feet. I just want—" I try to find the words to describe this feeling.

"You want peace before the baby comes," my mom says sagely, and I'm more relieved than I've ever been. "He's a good man, Summer. Let him be good to you."

"I SHOULD HAVE BROUGHT A BIGGER TRUCK." Dayton surveys the pile of gifts in the reception hall with a grin on his face. "These people must like you."

It's all lovely. All of it. But the size and shape of all these things makes anxiety rise into my throat. "They like me a little too much, I think."

Dayton puts his arm around me. "Don't worry about all of it," he says softly. "We'll go through it together."

"He's here!" My mom calls a greeting from the other end of the hall. All the other guests are gone. It's just me, Whit, my mom, and Dayton. "Summer, sit down. You look like you're about to have heat stroke. The rest of us will get this truck loaded."

I watch out the window as they carry boxes and bags of every size out to the bed of the pickup truck Dayton rented just for this occasion. My mom says something to him and he laughs. My heart aches. It's love and worry, all at once. I know we *made up* from our fight, but it still seems unresolved. Probably because that guy is still out there. And Dayton is still worried about it, even if he won't tell me.

He carries another bag out, and halfway to the truck the handles break, spilling tiny onesies on the sidewalk. Dayton is alone, his dark hair shining in the sun, and he bends carefully to the ground, maneuvering around his prosthetic, picking each one up like it's precious, irreplaceable.

Oh, my heart.

Those tiny clothes in his big hands.

Maybe he was right. Maybe I should quit. I'll be taking maternity leave once our daughter is born. What's the difference?

He stuffs the colorful onesies back into the bag and lifts it. Pain crosses his face as he stands up. Did he go to his appointment last week? Or did he reschedule it again?

I don't know that Whitney is beside me until she speaks. "Look at that," she says, and we both watch as Dayton crosses to the truck, opens the door, and tucks the bag carefully inside the cab. "He's going to be a great dad."

"Because he's being careful with the onesies?" It's a half-hearted joke.

She pats my shoulder and leans down to whisper into my ear. "Because he's *even* careful with the onesies."

32

SOMETHING IS STILL OFF between me and Summer. Not even the baby shower earlier today could dispel the tension between us.

I know exactly what it is.

It's Alexei.

That fucker is following us everywhere. He has to be. He knows where she works, but I don't want to scare her any more than she already is. I can't do that to her. I can't do that to the baby.

I bring in all the presents from the shower and stack the boxes in piles in the living room. She's waiting in the bedroom, her hair lit by the soft light, and in the dark hallway, I pause and look at her.

"Summer."

She turns from her spot at the foot of the bed. There's that look in her eyes. It's still there.

And yet...

She beckons to me, and as we climb onto the bed she pounces, tearing at my shirt and clothes. It's harder for her to do these days, now that her belly is so big, but she climbs on top of me and pushes me back against the pillows. I take her hips in my hands and devour her mouth. She breaks the kiss and bends to my collarbone, biting at the skin, leaving pinpricks of pain and passion across my chest.

I can't resist her.

She was irresistible before the pregnancy, and now, God's honest fucking truth, it's hard to look at her. Her body is *that* luscious with her glow. She's always soaking wet, and tonight is no exception.

Summer lifts her hips and lowers herself onto my hard length, her belly heavy between us. My cock twitches inside of her—fuck, she feels good. She closes her eyes and rolls her hips in slow circles, hands braced against my chest.

In the dim light of the bedroom, I can still see her face.

I knew it. Something's wrong.

Her mouth is pressed into a serious line, almost a frown. She's not panting with the usual enthusiasm and furious joy that normally overtakes her when we fuck.

I put my hand to her collarbone. "Stop."

Her body stills and she opens her eyes. "Why?"

"Are you enjoying this?"

She raises one eyebrow. "Yes. Are you?"

"You don't look like you're enjoying it."

"I look how I look." Summer tosses her head back.

I run the pad of my thumb over her cheek. "Look at me."

She lowers her eyes to meet mine.

"I said what I did last night in the heat of the moment. I was panicking. It was stupid. I never should have said it."

She casts her gaze down at my chest.

"Sunny, look at me."

Her blue eyes catch all the available light.

"I'm not leaving you, Sunny. I'll *never* leave you."

"Is it the right thing—" Her voice breaks. "Is it the right thing, to stay together?" She shakes her head, once, sharply. "Of course it's the right thing. I didn't—I mean, should we stay in the city? Should I quit my job?"

"No, and no." My resolve grows with every word that comes out of her mouth. I've been running from the past. I've been running from what happened with Alexei. I've been running longer than that. I've been running from what happened in that Humvee. And before that, I was running from my father, from the kind of man I never wanted to become. "I'm taking care of it."

"I want—"

"You want to know more, and I'll tell you everything." I inch my hand a little closer to her throat. She's not a breath play kind of girl, but the slightest pressure there is always rewarded with a gush of wetness between her legs. "But right now, you can relax. You can *forget*. Forget last night ever happened."

Her hands tense against my chest, gripping the hair there, when I reach between her legs, finding her clit beneath the fine, soft hair decorating her pussy. It's been a while since she felt good enough for a shave or a wax. The feel of it beneath my fingers makes me so hard that I'm excruciatingly aware of the blood rushing from my head to my cock.

I circle her clit, my hand close to where I'm inside her, and she gasps. "Do you promise?"

"Forget it *ever* happened," I growl into her ear. "And I promise I'll make you come until you beg me to stop."

I T TAKES a *lot* of orgasms to make Summer beg, but she does it at last, a final trembling wave moving through her body, a heaving, gasping moan.

Then she leans in, curling up against my side, and falls asleep without another word.

Her breathing is slow and even within seconds. I give it a few minutes before slipping from underneath the covers. Both of us could use a warm washcloth. I tend to myself in the bathroom and then heat a clean cloth, taking it back into the bedroom where Summer is sprawled across the bed. She stirs a little when I dip the cloth between her legs, murmuring something about how great I am.

Someday, she'll be right about that.

Once the washcloth is hung over the towel rack in the bathroom, I climb back into bed next to her. I fall instantly into a dream.

I'm in the Army, but it's not the same Army. Everything is different. The uniforms are all wrong, but the squad leaders are still assholes. I'm struggling to keep up. Where the hell is my prosthesis? I'm late for a drill and I look for it, realizing too late that I have both feet. Shit.

"Into the Humvee," someone shouts at me, so I climb in. Wes is in the driver's seat.

"I fucking hate you," he says. "You know what's going to happen, don't you?"

"Don't do this." I look out the front window, but I can't see shit. He shifts the Humvee into drive and we trundle away on the gravel road.

Wes drives with his teeth clenched, his eyes narrowed. He's not wearing his helmet. I try to tell him to put it on, but the words stick in my throat. I don't think we've gone far enough when he stops the Humvee and gets out.

"Wes!"

He's gone, but then he reappears at my door, yanking it open.

He's standing there with Alexei's wife.

"What are you—?"

He hauls me bodily out of the Humvee. I'm bigger than he is. I've always been bigger. It doesn't matter. I can't do anything to stop him.

"Here it is," he says. "Here's what you get, for being such a piece of shit." I scramble to get my feet underneath me as he pushes me forward, his fingers light on my shoulder blades.

I see it too late.

The land mine.

One of the ones re-buried by the Taliban after the Russians blanketed all of Afghanistan.

I feel the hard metal beneath my foot.

"Three, two, one," Wes counts, and the mine explodes.

AGONY. My foot is in agony.

It's both on fire and frozen, the pain all-consuming, and I react with my entire body. There's a strange howling. It takes me a second to realize what it is: it's me.

I grab for my left foot—anything to relieve the pain, anything, but it's not there.

I shout out a string of curses into the pillow. I don't know where I am. My vision is clouded red with pain.

"Day. Dayton."

There's another screaming twist of pain in my foot and I reach for it again, my hands scrabbling at the sheets.

"Dayton. Listen to my voice. Focus on my words." A gentle touch brushes against my shoulder. It feels far away.

"Straighten out your back."

I'm twisted, bent over in the bed, but I didn't know it until now. I grit my teeth and force myself upright, force my head back to the pillow.

The pillow in my bed.

I sense a palm against my forehead, the back of a hand against my cheek, whisper soft.

"You're at home in your bed," the voice says. "If you put your hand out, you can feel the sheets."

I stretch my hand out hesitantly. It takes a minute to register. There are sheets. There's no gravel path, no punishing heat. The sheets. Of my bed. At home.

"We're together at home. Your foot is hurting you, but you lost your foot during your deployment. It's not there anymore. Does that help?"

"No." It's the one word I can manage to say.

"Take in a deep breath and relax your legs." I fucking try. "I'm running my hands down your right knee, down your right shin." The hand follows the voice. A shifting on the bed.

"Now I'm going to run my hand down your left knee. And your left shin." The hand is on my knee, on my shin. "All the way down to your ankle. I'm putting my fingers around your ankle and squeezing, very gently."

"Fuck." The pain lessens by the slightest degree.

"I won't do that too long. Now my hand is on the top of your left foot. Very gentle. A slight pressure."

Where she touches, the pain recedes, enough that my mind clears along the edges.

"I'm going to bring my hand down to your toes. One, two,

three, four, five. And then to the bottom of your foot. Here's the ball of your foot. Here's the heel."

I resurface.

The pain swirls away, down to the dull ache that's my constant companion, and I push myself upright in the bed. Summer sits up straight, looking at me, her body still.

"Holy Christ."

She moves toward me, but her belly stops her. "Day?"

"Hey."

"Oh, my God." She crawls over my legs and curls up on my lap, letting out a quick breath. "You scared the shit out of me."

I can still feel the remains of the nightmare as it flees. "I scared the shit out of myself."

There's a pause.

"Are you okay?"

I take stock. I'm tired. It's the middle of the night. But nothing is extreme anymore. Sleep beckons at the boundaries of my mind. I lay back against the pillow, taking her with me. "You should be a counselor."

Summer shifts, curling into me. "You should see a real one."

I don't deserve a real counselor.

But—

"I'll do it," I tell her, as I fall back into what I hope is a dreamless sleep. "For you."

33

I WAKE up on the night-edge of dawn, my back against the hard line of Dayton's body.

Worry flashes in the corner of my mind, but then he breathes in and I know he's awake. Good. That means he's not having another nightmare. The air in the bedroom is tinged with a hint of gray light. I have the sense that time is moving slowly now. We can talk.

"Will you tell me what happened?"

He rolls over, his chest against my back, and puts a hand on my hip.

"When?"

"Between you and that guy."

Dayton runs his hand down to the angle of my knee and back up. "His name is Alexei Sokolov. Everybody calls him Alex."

I turn the name over in my mind. "Russian?"

"His parents were from Russia. They moved here when he was a kid. A little kid—I don't know exactly when."

Under any other circumstances, the warmth of Dayton's hand would either lull me to sleep or turn me on. This time, I hover in the feeling, in the sound of his voice.

"Why's he coming after you like this?" I don't say *after us*.

Dayton breathes in, his chest pressing against my back. In and out. In and out. "I was in rough shape when I got back from Afghanistan. I didn't come straight home after the incident in the Humvee."

"You didn't?" My entire body hums with anticipation. I've never heard these details before. Not from Wes. Not from anybody.

"No." Dayton's hand stops moving. We're approaching territory he doesn't want to talk about. "At first I was at a military hospital in Germany. Then I came back to Drum to wait out the end of my contract. By the time I got to the city, things were pretty dire."

"In terms of money?"

"In terms of *pain*." The word is loaded, heavy with the memory of his body thrashing beneath the sheets just a few hours ago. "My foot was gone, but it hurt all the time. The temporary prosthetic has *always* hurt."

"Why didn't you—"

"Because I didn't think I deserved a better one. It was my fault we ran over an IED in the first place."

"Dayton—"

"Do you want to know about Alexei or not?"

"Yes. God. He's trying to kill us." I hold the fear at bay by speaking the words in a light tone. This guy—he's come after me more than once.

Dayton pauses.

"When I got to the city, I crashed with a bunch of different people. A lot of them were ex-Army. Friends of friends, that kind of thing. For a while, I lived off savings and tried to dull the pain by getting drunk. Then money got tight and alcohol got expensive."

"Wait." I try to roll toward him, but it's too much effort, so I settle for putting my hand on his. "What about disability pay? The VA—"

Dayton laughs softly. "I didn't apply for any of that."

No. Of course he didn't.

"I met Alexei at a party. Curtis—the guy I was living with before this—had mutual friends in common. And Alexei had an offer."

My gut goes cold. "Day." I swallow before I can speak. "Did you kill someone?" Oh, God. If he killed someone, even out of desperation, how can I forgive him for that? Will I be able to forgive him for that?

"It wasn't like that," he says quickly, and then his body tenses against mine. "I didn't mean to."

My heart stops.

"What happened?"

"I was driving the car." Dayton takes his hand away and rolls away from me. "I was only driving the car."

Eighteen Months Ago

"I've got something that can take the edge off."

I look up through a haze of smoke and bullshit.

The guy has a crooked smile and he's too thin. His baseball cap is angled sideways. He looks like an idiot.

"Fuck off."

He doesn't fuck off. He sits down next to me on the couch. The cushion under his ass is worn through to the foam padding. "It hurts, doesn't it?" He jerks his jaw in the direction of my leg.

I don't want to talk about how much it hurts. I don't want to talk about the dull throb that settles into a stinging ache if I walk from the couch to the fucking bathroom. I don't want to talk about how *there is no fucking foot* but the toes feel cramped, curled under. I can't get them to release. And the throbbing guilt in the center of my chest. It's like a stab wound. If I had been paying attention...

"I can see it hurts," he says. "I promise. I can take the edge off."

"You can go away."

"Alex." Another guy cuts in from the side of the couch. "Delivery by three."

"I've got it," says the asshole who won't leave me alone. I guess his name is Alex. He turns his attention back to me. "Look. You give me a ride, I'll give you something that'll make it easier to handle." He's got an accent. It's faint, but it comes out in the consonants. "It'll be like the pain is on a separate island."

I look across the couch at him. Pale blue eyes. Light hair. I don't trust him.

The pain moves another inch up my leg. It's taking on more ground.

I am already ruined.

"One ride?"

He grins. "Maybe two. It's worth it, right?"

IT'S MORE than two rides.

After the first one, Alex presses two little pills into my hand and congratulates me. "You're about to be a new man."

He's right.

It doesn't erase the pain in my leg. It pushes it to a separate island, just like he said, across a river from my real life. For the first time since that day in the Humvee, I can think.

I think myself right into a neat little box, where what I'm doing for Alex is fine. I never ask him what he's doing at the houses we visit in the boroughs. I never look at the people he meets. I pick him up at his place and I drop him back off. That's it.

Sometimes, his wife comes along with us. She wears a thin silver band around her left ring finger and hardly speaks. Her name is Kate.

Alex pays me in pills, and in my newly clear-headed state, I figure out that I'm not going to be able to live on pills forever. So I take a job at Killon, manufacturing windows, and give him rides at night.

This has two effects. The first is that I'm fucking tired. The second is that the little pills don't work as well as they used to. I bargain with him. I need three. Then four.

On the sixteenth ride, I turn off the car when he gets in. Kate climbs into the backseat, the passenger side, and says nothing.

"What are you doing?" He shrugs his jacket up to his neck. "It's freezing out. Turn on the car."

"Pills first."

He shakes his head. "You know that's not how it goes."

"That's how it goes today." I'm banking on the fact that he doesn't have time before his delivery to get another ride. I'm banking on it because the pain has crawled all the way up into the back of my neck, an electric line from my foot to my head, and I can't think straight. I need the pills. It can't wait.

Alex sighs. "Two now, two after."

"All of them, right now."

He must hear the desperation in my voice because he reaches into his pocket for a folded napkin and drops them into my hand. One, two, three, four. I knock them back with the remains of a coffee I bought on the way out here. It's already cold.

I turn the car on.

"Where are we headed?"

He names a place on the Upper East Side and I sigh. It's almost two in the morning. This is going to take fucking forever.

We've only gone about fifteen blocks—still on the Queens side of the bridge—when a familiar *patter-patter* starts hitting on the top of the car.

Sleet.

Alex cranes his neck and looks out the window. "Shit."

"It's not good."

It's icy, coating the road and the windshield. At the next intersection, I tap on the brakes and the front wheels jerk sideways. I correct it, but it still takes longer than I expected to stop.

Alex has his hand on the door handle. "Fuck, man."

"It's fine."

This is his moment to call it off. I'm sure as hell not going to. I got what I came for, so I'm in no position to back out now. And even though I make it a point to know as little as possible about Alex, I've overheard some things. Namely that his full name is Alexei Sokolov, and he's got some shady fucking ties to a Russian underground group.

I push that fact out of my mind. I don't know anything.

We move through the intersection and the sleet intensifies. The pain in my leg is receding, moving out to low tide, and my head clears. The more it clears, the more I know one thing: we shouldn't be driving right now. It's the end of February, when the weather is volatile in New York City, and this kind of shit is no joke.

It's a long way from here to the Upper East Side.

A long fucking way.

I grip the wheel tighter and flick my eyes up to the rearview mirror. Kate sits in the back, staring out the window. What little light there is from the streetlights reflects off her face. She sits with her hands in her lap. Why does she go along with Alexei? On all the rides I've given him, she's gone on at least half, and she never gets out of the car.

The sleet pummels the road, the roof of the car, everything, and the wipers can't keep up. I stop at the next intersection and squint toward the stoplight. It looks red.

Kate says something from the backseat. I'm not paying attention, so I don't catch the words. I *do* catch that there's a note of alarm in her soft voice.

"It's going to be quick," Alexei says. "Then we'll go home."

I will the sleet to clear so I can see the fucking stoplight.

Is that a flicker of green?

Shit.

I wait.

It cycles through the colors again.

There—that must be yellow, and then red. It must be.

The sleet only gets heavier as we wait for green.

Alexei gets impatient, tapping his fingers on the dash.

I'm not totally sure it's changed when he brings his palms together, a sharp *clap*. "Let's go. Green light. Get out of here."

"I'm going."

I step on the gas and the car lurches forward into the intersection. It's a good thing it's so late. Minimal traffic.

Which is why it surprises me when the headlights blaze on the passenger side of the car.

"Fuck," Alexei yells. "*Fuck*."

I gun it, but the wheels scramble for purchase on the road. Military focus kicks in. I don't turn the wheel—that won't do us any good. We have to get out of here. We have to go forward. I stomp on the accelerator again but the wheels spin.

He doesn't see us.

He doesn't see us.

The lights bear down, one, two... I give one more desperate

step on the accelerator. The car careens forward. Kate screams.

It's not enough.

The truck—it's huge, it has to be a truck—slams into the back half of the car and we start spinning, a violent torque that slams my head against the driver's side window. I hear ragged breathing, the scraping of ruined metal, and then we collide with something. A building? A mailbox? The breathing cuts out in a gurgle that I'd recognize anywhere.

Alex sucks in a breath in the passenger seat and I pick up my head. Headache. Fuck. Something hot is on my cheek. I put my fingers to my cheekbone and they come away wet and red.

He's shouting something, but the sound rattles uselessly around in my brain. Alex shoves his full weight against the passenger door and it springs open. The sound of sleet gets louder. I watch him go to the back door, but the back door no longer exists in a way we'd think of as a door. It's crumpled into a mess.

So is Kate.

He dives back into the front and kicks me in the face on his way over the shitty center console. Sleet from his boots is everywhere.

In the backseat, he sits beside her, his chest heaving. He touches her face. He fumbles for her seatbelt and somehow gets it undone. Then, ever so gently, he puts his arm around her shoulder. When he pulls her body to him, her head lolls to the side like a broken doll.

She's gone.

"Kate," he breathes, and I look away. The sound of his voice is too intimate.

"Kate, it's all right." He takes a deep breath. "Kate?"

I open the door and half-slip, half-stumble out of the car.

I'm halfway down the block, dialing 9-1-1, when I hear Alexei start to howl.

35

SUMMER

DAY DOESN'T SAY MUCH the morning after he tells me about the car accident.

He brings me coffee, half-caf with all the cream and sugar he can fit in the cup, and then he goes back to the kitchen. He reappears with a plate of scrambled eggs and toast as I'm getting out of the shower.

It's a process, with a big belly like this. I'm constantly off-balance. I feel even more off-balance today, after all the events of last night. Highs and lows. I still have an emotional hangover from hearing Dayton talk about that accident.

And it *was* an accident. I believe that with every inch of my being.

He doesn't.

I eat breakfast in bed, wearing just my panties, while he gets dressed for work.

I watch his reflection in the mirror by the dresser while he buttons his shirt. "You have an appointment today, don't you?"

His eyes flick down to the floor and back up. "Yeah."

"Do you want me to come?"

A darker expression moves over his face like a shadow. I brace myself for him to say *no, I don't want you to go anywhere. I want you to stay inside this house with the doors locked and call the police if anyone so much as knocks.*

"You have work." He meets my eyes in the mirror. "You're right. They need you there. I know you'll be safe."

I put down the piece of toast I've been eating and shimmy to the side of the bed. Day is there as soon as I move, holding his hand out for support. I hug him the moment I'm on my feet. He seems tentative somehow.

I squeeze him tighter.

"What's this for?" I hear the smile in his voice, even with my cheek pressed to his chest.

"It's so you know."

"So I know what?"

"That everything's going to be all right."

He sighs, but the tension is still there, holding his core hostage. "I love you, Sunny."

How many times has he said this to me? I don't know. It doesn't matter. It still fills me with a sparkling excitement, like it's the very first time.

I only wish there was nothing to mar it. No black cloud. No

image creeping in the back of my mind of Dayton's hands on the wheel. Was he high from whatever was in those pills? He shouldn't have been driving that car, not while taking painkillers.

He calls for a car to take me into work. I should be taking the subway, but the stairs make my ankles hurt, so I am delivered to the front door of my office in the city's finest Uber each morning.

On the way, I watch the traffic and think about that man's wife.

Alexei was *definitely* doing something shady. Delivering drugs? Probably. But love doesn't care if someone's doing something shady. Or, in Dayton's case, allegedly doing something shady. I should know. And I'm the last person who wants to encourage being on the wrong side of the law.

All that has no bearing on Kate, the silent woman in the backseat. Why was she with Alex? Why did she ride along that day?

There's a simple answer to that.

She was in love with him.

I wish Dayton was in the car with me right now.

Baby kicks and rolls, and I breathe out, giving her more room.

That's when it hits me, like one of her big kicks.

Kate was somebody's baby, too.

This little girl isn't even born yet, but already I can feel the hole she'd leave in the universe if she was gone.

Kate was that person for someone. For how many people? Was Alex the only one orbiting her so closely? Where were her parents? How did they find out about the accident? The closest I've ever come to that feeling are those moments when I thought Wes might have died in Afghanistan.

I cannot cry in this Uber.

"You okay?" The driver's eyes regard me with concern in the rearview mirror. I'm sure he's terrified that I'll go into labor in his personal vehicle.

I give him a broad smile. "Lost in thought."

"Something sad?"

"Oh," I say, looking out the window as he accelerates. "I heard some sad news last night."

"Sorry to hear that," he answers awkwardly.

"It's okay."

Within a couple of minutes, we're at Heroes on the Homefront.

At my desk, I sit heavily in my rolling chair and pull up the schedule for the day. I have a few appointments scheduled for the late morning. Until then, it's paperwork central.

Dayton's face, looking out at me from a picture frame near my monitor, catches my eye.

In the picture, he's seventeen, standing on the end of the dock at the cottage in Michigan. His dark hair is windswept, and his skin is tan against the bright red of his swimsuit. He's not quite smiling, but there's such laughter in his eyes that you could see a grin there. There's not a single tattoo on his skin. The future was still waiting for him.

I dug out the photo right after we moved in together from a box I kept hidden in the back of my closet for all those years.

I look at seventeen-year-old Day and try to reconcile him with the man he is now. Is he still a good man despite the things he's been part of? I knew when he deployed that he'd kill people. He had no other choice. It was a war, and that was his job.

But what about Kate?

It was an accident. He didn't plan that late-night outing. He didn't plan the sleet, the ice, the truck.

A small voice in the back of my mind won't relent. *He didn't fight against it, either. He could have refused. He could have stopped at any time.*

The baby kicks three times, a jaunty rhythm that seems to say *hey, idiot, snap out of it.*

She's right. I love him even if he shouldn't have been behind the wheel that night. God knows he's paid the price. He's *still* paying it. And beyond that, I spend all day talking to veterans just like him who are gripped by pain that nobody can begin to understand. Who am I to judge?

It wasn't right. He wasn't doing the right thing.

It's a nagging thought, and I hate it.

The baby flips over and starts hiccupping.

I spend all day helping people like Dayton. Maybe, in the

grand scheme of things, everything I do will cancel out the mistakes he made.

"That's stupid," I say out loud, but I can't help giving seventeen-year-old Day a wistful glance. Things were so much simpler then.

I LIED TO SUMMER.

Again.

It's a lie of omission, but it's still a fucking lie.

The guy who drove Alex around the city, never looking at the houses they drove to, would have had no problem with lying. He'd have said there's always a gray area.

How times have changed.

Still, there's no way in hell I'm going to worry her with this.

I left work two hours before my appointment. They don't have any idea how long a prosthetic fitting is going to take, so I fudged it. I'm taking most of the morning and part of the afternoon off. That doesn't feel great either, but there's only one solution to the problem of Alexei stalking us around the city.

I have to confront him.

Not *confront* him. Meet him. Talk to him, at least. Maybe, if I can get him on neutral ground, we can have a conversation.

I don't have a way to contact him.

But I know who does.

I take the train to Queens and walk to my old apartment, the heat settling thickly on my shoulders. It's too hot for this and my leg aches in the prosthesis. I have the ugly sensation that I'm being watched, and I'm probably right. In this kind of neighborhood, people are always watching.

The hallway of the apartment building is fragrant with the pungent odor of garbage and spilled beer. I can't believe Summer came here to visit me and still wanted to be with me after that.

Small miracles.

I'm planning to knock on Curtis's door, but when I raise my hand to the battered wood, I see there's no need.

It's already open a couple inches.

I don't like that.

I push it out of the way and step inside.

It's dark inside, and so silent my stomach tightens at the lack of sound. Every muscle is on alert. Is he here? Is he dead? Was this place robbed? What am I walking into? I should turn around and go right back out. I don't.

The only light is coming in from the gaps around the curtains, letting in sharp morning sunlight. My prosthetic bangs against something on the floor. A beer can clatters off to the side. As my eyes adjust, I see that the entryway and the living room are more of the same. He had a party here recently.

"Curtis?" I call out his name and blink, taking in more of the wreckage. It's looking less like a party and more like a downward spiral with every step I take.

There's a slow shuffling from the second bedroom and I follow the sound.

"Curt, it's me."

The same darkness cloaks the bedroom, but the curtains are shitty here, too. Curtis is curled up on a bare mattress on the floor. He's fully dressed, down to his shoes. He's got a towel over his shoulders like a blanket.

"Curtis."

He blinks. His face is on display in one of the lines of light from the window, and his eyes are so sunken in it makes my stomach turn.

"Day." His voice is ragged, torn to shreds. "How'd you get in?"

"The door was open."

He pushes himself upright, and I can see in the movement that he's not okay. Something falls softly to the floor with a delicate *click*. A needle.

Curtis stares toward the window. "What time is it?"

I pull out my phone and check the screen. "Just past eleven-thirty."

"Shit." He runs a hand through his hair. It hasn't been

washed in quite some time. "Guess it doesn't matter, though."

"Are you still working?"

He laughs out loud. "No, man. No. Why would you think I could hold down that type of job?"

"I thought things were going okay at Killion."

"Killion?" His grin is crazy, misshapen. "That was three fucking jobs ago. You probably don't remember what that's like. What do you do now, sit on your ass in an office? Collared shirt, look at you."

"Get up." I haul him bodily off the mattress and put him on his feet. "This is—" I shake my head. "You can't live like this."

Curtis pushes my hands away. "Why are you here?"

I don't bother lying. "Do you have Alex's number?"

He looks to the side and breathes out, a short sigh of disappointment. "It's in my phone somewhere. In the other room. If that's still his number."

I go out to the living room and throw the curtains open. This place is in worse shape than I thought. Jesus, Curtis. He's going to die in here if he doesn't do something.

If *I* don't do something.

The phone is buried in the middle of some rotting takeout boxes on the coffee table. Curtis trails out of the bedroom while I flip through his address book.

"Did you find it?"

"Yeah."

I enter the number in my phone.

"I'm going to give you a number, too. The first thing you're going to do when I walk out of here is to call this place."

He snorts. "What place?"

"Heroes on the Homefront."

"Oh, fuck that. Those people don't know—"

I turn to face him and shove his phone into his hand. "You're killing yourself. Do you get that? You are *killing* yourself."

Curtis's eyes go wide, then they darken. His next words are soft. "Who cares, man? I can't do these jobs. I can't fucking sleep at night. The dreams—"

I look him in the eye. "I know. Trust me. I know."

He drops his gaze to the floor.

"I'll let them know to expect a call from you." I check the time on my phone. "By noon. If you don't call, I'm coming back here."

"You can't—"

"I *can,* asshole."

He hears the promise in my voice.

"I'll call."

"Good." I head for the door. The fitting is in the city, so I'm traveling back there. "I'm also going to send somebody to clean this place up. Call. Shower." I point my fingers at him. "Don't let me down."

∼

I PULL the brand new liner over my leg and take a deep breath.

My heart's *racing*.

I didn't expect to feel this way, getting a new prosthetic, but I do.

Dr. O'Connors balances it in front of my stool until I'm done with the liner, then hands it over.

"Should be a perfect fit," he says, his eyes on the socket. "But if it's not, we can make adjustments."

I slide my leg in and stand up.

Oh my God.

There's no pain.

It fits.

It fits.

My missing toes uncurl and relax for the first time in months.

"I—"

I take a few steps forward. Dr. O'Connors' assistant, Sherry, pokes her head in the door and gasps. It scares the hell out of me.

"What's wrong?"

"Dayton!" Her face is alight. "You're so *tall*!"

Joy. A pure, undeserved joy ignites in the center of me,

followed by a stab of regret. Summer should have been here for this. I can feel it in my shoulders. I've been standing off-balance for so long that I stopped noticing. Now my back is straight.

There is no pain.

"Show me the walk!"

I walk in a circle around the exam room again. Sherry turns over her shoulder and calls down the hall. "Guys! Come see Dayton!"

A little crowd of nurses in scrubs gathers at the door as Dr. O'Connors puts me through my paces. Every exercise is a breeze. There's *no pain.*

When he stands up and pronounces it *absolutely perfect,* all of the nurses clap.

Dr. O'Connors puts a hand on my shoulder. "I'm glad you finally showed up for this."

I give him a look. "How old are you, even?"

"Same age as you."

Everyone laughs, and then we move seamlessly into end-of-appointment nonsense. Scheduling the check-up. Things I should watch for. All that.

The nurses start to disperse.

"Wait." Sherry stops at the door. "I need your help with one last thing."

37

SUMMER

My phone rings in my purse, for the third time.

"I'll check in with you tomorrow," I tell the veteran sitting across from me, one Frederick Brown, and move to stand.

"Don't get up," he says with a grin. We shake hands over my desk while I'm still sitting down.

As soon as he's out in the hall, I grab for my phone.

It's a FaceTime call.

Dayton? Using *FaceTime?*

I swipe to answer the call and run a hand over my hair. I wasn't counting on *this*.

The call connects, and the image widens onto the screen. It's not Dayton's face. It's the floor of what looks like the VA hospital. Then the sound cuts in.

"—oh, sorry, I don't know—" The camera swings upright, and there he is.

"Hey, Sunny," he says.

I stare.

I can't help it.

What's different?

He's standing so *tall*. He's standing so *well*.

"Oh my God, Day, is that your new prosthetic?"

"Yeah."

He's beaming.

"Show me!"

The camera backs up, and Day takes a few strides down the hall and back again.

I can't help the delighted squeal that escapes my throat, and he laughs.

"Doesn't it look good?"

"You look *great*," I tell him, and that's when I get choked up. How could I not? I didn't know how much the pain weighed him down, dipped his shoulders, until this moment. "I'm so happy for you, honey."

He steps closer, and then the camera flips around to show his face. "Don't cry. Sherry's here. She was holding the phone." He lifts the phone away from his face and there's one of the nurses from the hospital, waving. She has tears in her eyes, too.

"Hi, Summer," she says, and wipes at one of them. "Cry all you want. It's an amazing sight, isn't it?"

"Yes, he is." I go through so many tissues it's unbelievable. Today is going to be no exception, clearly.

Day rolls his eyes, but they're still lit up by his happiness. "I'll show you at home, okay?"

I want to make a sex joke, but I don't know if Sherry's still close. "You'd better."

"Hey." The light changes. He must be moving down the hall. "You remember my old roommate?"

I *barely* remember his old roommate. He was too thin, and I saw him for twenty seconds on my single visit to the apartment. "Yeah?"

"He's a vet, too." Concern flashes across Dayton's face. "I saw him today. I told him to give you guys a call. Has he called yet?"

Carla pokes her head in the door. "Message for you." She puts the paper on my desk and tiptoes out, smiling.

I look down at the yellow slip. "Curtis Howard?"

Day looks relieved. "That's him."

"I'll call him back right now."

He nods. "Good. That's good."

"I love you."

Another smile that melts my core. "I love you. See you at home."

CURTIS IS IN BAD SHAPE.

I can tell by the way he sounds when he answers the phone. His voice is hoarse, trembling, and my heart goes out to him.

"I didn't want to call," he says with a sigh after I introduce myself.

"I'm glad you did," I tell him. "We can offer you a variety of services, from job placement to treatment programs."

"Oh, Jesus."

I keep it professional. "Can I tell you more about those things? Do you have a minute?"

"You can," he says, but a heartbeat later, he adds, "but I'm not going to remember anything you say over the phone."

"That's no problem." This poor guy. "Would you be willing to come in tomorrow for a quick meeting? We can go over all of this in person and make some decisions about what you want to do."

"I guess." He lets out a short, barking laugh. "Day said he'd come back here himself if I didn't call. I'm guessing he'll do the same if I don't meet with you."

"I'd take him at his word," I say briskly, and he laughs, the sound more genuine this time. "How about one o'clock? Is that too early?"

"That's fine," he says, a note of concern in his voice. "Are you far from the subway station?"

"No. Not far." I think of Dayton walking here on that old prosthetic of his, that very first day. "I'll text you the directions."

"Sounds good."

"See you at one."

DAYTON'S HAND is beneath my belly, angling toward my clit, when I stop him.

I have to stop him *now*, because the moment he gets his fingers down there, I won't be able to concentrate on conversation. We're lying beneath the blankets, the air conditioning unit blowing directly onto the bed.

"You're not in the mood?"

"I'm in the mood." I kiss him, ending with a little nip on his bottom lip. "I have a question."

"Ask away." He smells so good, fresh out of the shower, that I wish I had the energy to stay up all night with him.

"What made you go see your friend today?"

Dayton blinks, his forehead wrinkled. "I needed something from him."

Worry draws a finger down the back of my spine, but Dayton inches his hand downward and pleasure overtakes it. "If I ask you what that was, will you tell me?"

"No."

"Fine."

"Don't be upset."

I spread my legs under the blankets. I'm propped up on two pillows because I can't sleep any other way, but I still feel Dayton over me.

"I'm not upset. I'm worried about him, though. He sounded..."

"He's a wreck."

"I'm glad you told him to call."

"I knew you'd help him."

"I'm going to try, but—"

"You're the best there is, Sunny. Was there anything else?"

"No, I—"

He holds his hand still. "You what?" Day's voice is teasing, warm.

"I can't remember." I whisper the words and close my eyes.

Dayton kisses my neck, once, twice, three times. By the third kiss, I'm trembling. "Keep your legs spread like that. I love it."

He strokes his fingers between my legs, sending heat down to my toes. I raise my arms over my head and grip the head-board. One more stroke, and I'm lost to his touch.

38

AT MID-MORNING, the heat is verging on oppressive, but I couldn't make this call at home.

I'm not making it in the office, either.

I'm around the corner from the building outside a café. This walk would have *hurt* yesterday morning. Today, it's nothing. *Nothing.*

Why did I wait so long?

The answer is in my phone. I saved the number under his initials. I don't know why.

I bring up the contact and press *call* before I can drag it out any longer.

One ring.

Two.

And then...

"Hello."

His voice is flat but unmistakable.

"Alex."

He sucks in a breath. He knows it's me.

"Dayton Nash," he says slowly. "I can't fucking believe you'd call."

"Yeah, well—" I move past the café and flatten my back against the brick wall. That, at least, is solid, unlike the ground beneath my feet. "I have a phone now."

He laughs, a cruel note in his voice. "How times have changed."

Enough of this. "I want to talk to you."

"We're talking."

"I want to talk to you in person." That car, coming up over the curb, right at Summer. Right at our baby. "I think it's time we discussed what happened."

"Oh?"

I tighten my grip on the phone. "That was the past. Summer —" Shit. I didn't mean to say her name. Too late now. "She has nothing to do with that. You can't keep coming after her."

"Who's going to stop me?"

"Alex, she had *nothing* to do with it. If you want your revenge, you can take it out on me. In person. Stop chasing us around the city. She's pregnant, for fuck's sake." The rage builds, but I keep my voice level. I have to control it. I *have* to control it.

Alex is silent on the other end of the line.

"Come on. You've been trying to run me over with your car. Sit down with me and talk instead. I'll buy you a beer."

He's not going to agree to it. He's going to hang up, and then I'll be fucked. I'm *already* fucked. This is a last-ditch, desperate attempt at heading off the inevitable, and we both know it.

"Fine."

"What?"

"I said, fine. I'll meet you." He laughs again, like this is the most absurd thing that's ever happened in his life. That can't possibly be true. "Where do you want to meet?"

Why the hell is he letting me choose? It's all wrong, but I've got him on the phone. I've come this far. I name a bar a few blocks from the office. It's a shit place, which should be perfect for a guy like Alex.

"What time are you free for our little date?" Goosebumps rise up on the backs of my arms, and I look around without turning my head. Is that fucker here right now? I wouldn't put it past him.

"One o'clock."

"See you then, sweetheart."

~

I'M ALMOST BACK to the office when I realize it.

I have another call to make.

The old Dayton would have walked into this meeting with nobody.

The new Dayton has a woman to go home to and a baby on the way. I can't walk in there by myself. I don't know what I'm going to say to Alex, but even if I say the right things, he still might lose his shit.

Wes answers on the first ring.

"This is Wes Sullivan." His voice is clipped and precise.

"Where are you?"

He makes a noise in the back of his throat at the sound of my voice. "That's a personal question, don't you think?"

"Are you on base?" If he's on base, I'm screwed. It's a six-hour drive in the middle of the day.

There's the sound of traffic in the background. Is it from my end or his? "No." A gust of wind whistles in my ear, and then it's quieter.

"Where are you?"

"I'm in Newark."

"For *what*?"

"For some leave time." Wes doesn't bother to hide his irritation. "Which you're interrupting with this asinine phone call. What do you want?"

I step to the inside of the sidewalk and hold the phone tighter to my ear. "I don't know why the hell you'd vacation in Newark, but I'm fucking glad."

"Why are you—?"

"I need your help."

There's a long silence.

"Listen." I take a deep breath. "I'm sorry I got us blown up in that Humvee. Okay? I'm fucking sorry about it. But there's some shit happening and I need you for back-up."

"You didn't get us blown up."

This is news. "*What*?"

"That wasn't your fault." Wes is incredulous. "Nobody could have predicted that IED. It was my fault, if it was anyone's." He lets out a bitter laugh. "Should have seen it coming. And now you're missing a fucking foot."

I listen hard to what he's saying right now, like I'm missing something *other* than a foot. "You've hated me all these years for that fucking IED."

Wes sighs. "I didn't *hate* you, you asshole. I didn't want a scumbag like *me* spending time with my sister. Or thinking about her. I know what you're like. You're my best friend." Another pause. "Dumbshit."

"Can you come here or not?" I give him the address of where to meet me. "I need you there at twelve-thirty."

"That's an hour and a half from now."

"Then you have thirty extra minutes to jerk off, if that's what you want to do."

"You're very charming, Dayton. Did anyone ever tell you that?"

"Lots of people. Are you going to be there?"

"Have I ever let you down?"

We let that ruminate in the air between us.

"I'll be there," he says finally, and ends the call.

I want to go home.

More than anything in the world, I want to go home.

My back is *killing* me, and even Hazel's box of doughnuts isn't making me want to stay at work today. From today, it's four weeks to my due date.

"I got you a glazed twist," Hazel says, lifting up the doughnut on a little paper plate. She holds it up high, like it's a precious jewel, then laughs and brings it to my desk.

I smile up at her and rest my arms on my belly. "Thanks. I didn't have the will to lug myself all the way to your office."

She nods wisely. "Next door *is* pretty far away. If I was in your state, I'd never get out of my chair."

"Seriously."

"You look tired."

"I *am* tired." The baby belts out a hard kick, shoving herself upward into my ribs, and I let out a breath that makes Hazel raise her eyebrows. "It's an all-night party in there."

"You know..." She looks from side to side like she's telling me classified information. "I don't think anyone would mind if you left early. We can cover for you."

"That sounds—" It sounds *amazing.* It sounds like the world's greatest gift. I know they're good for it, too. Heroes on the Homefront is my dream job. I sigh. "It sounds perfect, but I have an appointment at one that I can't miss."

Hazel clicks her tongue. "You're too dedicated, my friend."

"I'll sneak out after that."

"Good idea. Honestly, you look great, but...you also look miserable. I mean that in the nicest way. You're so gorgeous."

I laugh and so does she. "It's the sentiment that counts."

"Need anything else? Bottle of water from the fridge?"

"You're an angel. Kind of. But you're very devilish, too. I mean that in the nicest way."

Hazel laughs out loud while she fetches the water, drops it off at my desk, and then goes back to her own office.

I plan out the rest of my day. She's right—I *am* miserable, and I need to go home. It's not a defined misery, really. I don't feel *bad,* just...overwhelmingly heavy. Most of all, I want to be in my apartment. Specifically, I want to be in my bed. I'm not normally a bed person, unless you count the many, many days I could spend there with Dayton, but today is different. Today I feel a powerful pull toward my clean, white sheets. I don't even care about sleeping. I only want to be snuggled up in the bed.

It's weird.

I glance again at the clock. Fifteen minutes until one.

I've gathered all the possible preliminary paperwork we'll need. I'm going to knock this one out of the park. So what if I'm exhausted? I saw the worry in Dayton's eyes when he talked about Curtis. The guy must be in bad shape.

This is the perfect place for him to come.

I stack the papers up in a neat pile on my desk and review my talking points. If he needs rehab, I've got two standing by to take him. If he needs housing, I have an apartment manager in Brooklyn that's got a one-bedroom available. If he wants to go to school, I've got options for that, too. I've even got a couple of job openings on hand to mention.

"You're killing it," I tell myself, then pick up the glazed twist. I haven't been very hungry this morning, which is strange, but the moment the sugary glaze touches my lips, I'm ravenous. I wolf down the doughnut.

When I'm done inhaling the sugary confection, I look down at my belly, encased in my finest maternity tank, the silky fabric as business-casual as I could get.

I'm a mess.

There are glaze shards everywhere.

My soul longs to be in my own bed, where I could brush the crumbs onto the sheets with no one the wiser. I wash the sheets every weekend, so who cares?

I heave myself up from my desk chair and waddle past Hazel's office. She whips around in her chair at the sound of my footsteps. "Are you leaving?"

"No." I gesture to my shirt. "I ate that doughnut like a total savage."

"Do you want another one?"

I have a long way to go to the bathroom, and if I'm going to minimize the number of trips—

"Sure." I sit down in her office and let her fawn over me. This one's chocolate with chocolate frosting. She has one, too. We both eat in silence until the doughnuts are gone.

"Do you have to pee constantly?" Hazel asks, eyeing my belly.

"More or less. But it's a battle, because I don't want to walk all the way to the bathroom and back."

"How much longer do you have?"

"A month."

She shakes her head in solidarity. "That's a long time."

"No shit."

That makes her laugh. "You want company?"

"If you're going that way."

"Come on, girl. You've got fifteen minutes left until your meeting. Let's do this."

By the time she drops me off back at my office, I'm energized. "Thanks for the doughnuts."

Hazel grins. "I better not see you for very long tomorrow, either."

"We'll see."

She gives me the thumbs-up and goes back to her desk.

I settle in behind my desk, feet aching from the walk down the hall. It's all going to be worth it. For the baby, of course, but today in particular is going to be worth it. I can already picture Dayton's face when I tell him about his friend's new options, how I connected with him during the meeting, how he left with a new lightness in his step and a head full of plans for the future.

Day will probably be *so* proud that he insists on taking me somewhere delightful, like the bed. It's so hot that the air conditioner can hardly keep up, but he'll help me strip off this tank top and the stretchy bra underneath. I won't even have to take my own pants off. And even though I'm roughly the size of a blue whale, his dark eyes will burn with intensity when he sees me naked.

His hands on me...God, I want his hands on me right this moment. He likes to put his palms on my belly and wait for baby girl to kick, but even more than that, he likes—

"Summer?" Carla raps her knuckles on my doorframe. "You're one o'clock is here."

I stand up from my chair too fast, trying to cover the naughty thoughts I've *definitely* been thinking about Dayton. "Thanks, Carla." A little bit of heat clings in my cheeks and I press at them with my fingertips, willing them to go away.

Carla turns and looks over her shoulder. Her smile is her standard welcoming smile, but there's something in it that makes me think *oh, no.* Curtis must be having a rough day.

"Come on in," she says to Curtis, beckoning him down the hall. "Summer's office is right here." She looks back in on me and I mouth *thank you.* She's been bringing clients back to my office all week so I don't have to get up as much. I should get her a gift card to Sephora. She loves that place.

There's a muffled *thanks.* Carla nods her head, gives me a little wave, and steps out of view.

Curtis comes in and I take a deep breath. It's hot, but he's wearing a black hoodie and his gaze is pinned to the floor. "Hi, Curtis. Welcome to Heroes on the Homefront. I'm Summer Sullivan, and—"

He raises his head.

It's not Curtis.

"I know you who are." A cruel grin spreads across his face. He reaches behind him and closes the door with a *click* that seems terribly, terribly final. "Have a seat. We're going to talk."

40

"I'M NOT SAYING I *like* it." Wes grimaces into his beer. "I'm saying...I can accept it. For now." He looks me in the eye. "But if you ever hurt her, I'll—"

"I got it."

We're tucked into a dingy side booth at the bar. I've got a clear view of the door, and from the entryway, you can't see if there's a second person in the booth. To say I'm tense would be an understatement of ridiculous proportions. I'm riding the fine edge between sharp adrenaline focus and an urgent need for action, and here's Wes, lecturing me about how I'm supposed to treat his sister.

I let my eyes wander over the bar and move the conversation along. It's one o'clock now. Alexei isn't here. In another minute, he'll be late. "You still thinking about getting out?"

Wes follows my gaze, doing his own check on the space. Between the two of us, there's no way we're missing anything. "Yeah, I—" He shakes his head, his jaw tightening. "Things haven't been the same since that day."

"I'm exactly the same."

Wes laughs at the joke, but the look in his eyes is serious. "I should have gotten out when you did."

"No reason to. It was still working for you."

He scoffs. "It's not working anymore. The nights—" His voice cuts off abruptly and looks back down into his beer. He gives a short shake of his head and then lifts it to his mouth and takes a deep swig.

Wes doesn't need to say anything more. I know about the nights.

But we're here in broad daylight now, and there's a more pressing issue: Alexei still isn't here.

I check the time and *snap,* I'm back on full alert.

Not only is Alexei not here, I don't have the feeling he's *going* to be here.

Wes shifts in his seat. "One o'clock, right?"

"Yes."

I told him the Cliffs Notes version of the story, leaving out the parts where Alexei came after Summer. *That* would have had him on the hunt for this guy, and that's the last thing anybody needs.

"He's late."

"Yeah."

Wes looks out across the bar again. "Something's not right."

The bar itself isn't right. It's a shitty place, mostly empty, though it's the middle of the afternoon, so I wasn't expecting a crowd. The bartender leans against the bar, staring at his phone.

My own phone rings. It's the number for Heroes on the Homefront. Oh, shit. I don't want to lie to Summer about this, but what if something's happening? This late in the pregnancy, the chance of baby-related events goes up every minute.

"Are you going to get that?"

"Watch the door." Wes turns dutifully toward the front of the bar, his knees poking out of the booth. I pick up the phone and swipe to answer the call. "Hello?"

"Dayton? Mr. Nash?"

The voice on the other end of the line is shaken, almost breathless. It's not Summer.

"This is." It sounds like the receptionist. Shit. What's her name?

"This is Carla calling from Heroes on the Homefront." Her voice is trembling, panicked. "Mr. Nash, I—" She can't get the words out.

I stand up from the table, and even though my fist is clenched tightly around the phone, even though my shoulders are pricking with icy goosebumps, I marvel at how it feels to stand up with no pain. "Carla, take a deep breath."

She obeys, her breath hissing into the phone.

"What's going on?"

"Dayton, we have a situation at the office." She sounds

marginally more even-keeled, but all I need is information. I snap my fingers in front of Wes's face. He's on his feet in an instant.

I head for the door of the bar.

Fuck Alexei.

Fuck this meeting.

If something's happening to Summer—

I twist around. Wes tosses a twenty onto the surface of the table and follows me, his mouth set in a grim line.

"Okay. What's the situation?"

"Summer—she—" And then there it is from Carla, a muffled, terrified sob.

I choke back an irritation bordering on rage. "Carla, you need to tell me what's happening. I can be there in twenty minutes. Or I can go to the hospital. Tell me what's happening."

She takes a shuddering breath. "She had an appointment at one o'clock. The man—I think his name is Curtis—has shut himself in her office."

This makes zero sense.

"Is she with him?"

"He says he's got a gun, Dayton."

I have a moment of vertigo as I shove my way out onto the sidewalk into the heat. The sidewalk sways beneath me and Wes's hand comes down hard on my shoulder, holding me up.

"He won't let anyone in. He won't let her out."

"I'll be there in twenty minutes."

I end the call with a furious stab.

"What's happening?"

Guilt and fury cascade down the length of my spine. This is *my* fault. I never should have let her go to the office alone. I should have made her stay home. I should have stayed the fuck away from her when I had the chance to—

"Day!" Wes's voice is sharp and clear. "Snap out of it. What's happening?"

"Alexei. He's not here, because he's at Summer's office. He's taken her hostage."

The blood drains from Wes's face, his expression hardening into something so deadly the hairs on the back of my neck stand up.

Then he turns on his heel and steps directly out into the traffic. I can't believe that anyone would stop for him, with a look like that on his face, but seconds later a yellow cab pulls up to the curb. Wes turns back to me and I feel myself *shift*. The panic melts away, and all that's left is a steely determination.

I don't care if I die. All I care about is getting to Summer.

Wes climbs into the back of the cab and beckons me in beside him. "Give him the address," he barks.

I recite the address to him, then bring my hand down hard on the back of the seat. "Let's go. Let's *go*."

41

SUMMER

I FEEL every beat of my heart.

I'm so afraid right now, that I feel as if the fear has split off from my body and is hovering in the corner of the room, watching me, watching this situation unfold.

There I am, seated at my desk at Heroes on the Homefront, sweating slightly in my sleeveless maternity tank top, staring across at a man who might kill me.

I recognize the outline of his face from the car that drove up onto the sidewalk. I know his voice. He's raised it once to shout out the door to the others in the office that if anyone comes in here, he'll kill me. "I have a gun," he said, though I haven't seen it. He could be hiding it anywhere under that black hoodie of his.

I've already done the logistics. There is a desk between me and the door. There are two chairs. And there is one very dangerous man sitting in one of the chairs.

There is no way out.

When he focuses his attention back on me, I feel like I'm watching from above, talking to him, trying to remain calm and rationalizing.

"Alexei. That's your name, isn't it?"

He leans back in the chair. "Summer Sullivan." His eyes flick down to my belly. "You're fucking huge now."

As if in response to the comment, my entire belly tightens, every muscle pulling downward. There's an ache bearing down at the center of my pelvis like a cramp. It tenses, then releases. There's no *way* he's doing this to me. I let out a breath that I wasn't even aware I was holding in.

"I'm pretty pregnant, yeah."

A slow shake of his head makes the summer light reflect off his reddish-colored hair. "Why would a girl like you fuck a guy like him?"

"Like who?" Instinct. It's pure instinct. If I can keep him talking, then he might not shoot me. If I can keep him talking, there's time for someone to open the door and end all this.

Alexei's mouth twists into an ugly scowl. "You know who I'm talking about. Don't act like a dumb bitch."

I smile at him, hoping the expression looks indulgent rather than terrified. "For all you know, I've been sleeping around."

His eyes widen in surprise, and then he laughs. "I don't think so. Why would Dayton let someone as pretty as you out of his sight?" He puts on an exaggerated frown. "Oops. He shouldn't have done that."

My belly flexes again, a crushing tension, and I sit up as straight as I can. It does nothing to relieve the pressure.

After a few moments, it goes away. "He doesn't come to work with me," I say lightly. It's all I can think to do. I'm going to steer this into a normal meeting. Maybe it'll throw him off. Maybe. "What's your priority this year, Alexei?"

He narrows his eyes and sits up, mirroring my posture. "My priority?"

"Yes." I cock my head to the side. "What is the one thing you want to accomplish by the end of the year? It's September, so you've got a solid four months until you'll need to come up with some new goals for next year."

He stares, his gaze astute and calculating. "Are you fucking kidding me?"

"No." I fold my hands over my belly. "I'm asking. What's your main goal?"

Confusion clouds his features. "I told you to stop acting like a dumb bitch."

I let the slightest hint of irritation show. "If you're not going to answer my questions, then stop wasting my time. I've got another appointment coming up in just a few minutes."

Alexei's face clears, as if he's realizing for the first time exactly what he's gotten himself into. Right now, he's left himself two choices: shoot me or leave. If he gets up and walks out now, who knows what'll happen? The police could be waiting to shoot *him*.

He leans forward and brings his clenched fists down on the surface of my desk. Hard. It takes everything I have not to flinch. My belly compresses again, the pressure even more painful this time. What the *fuck*—

"I haven't slept."

I blink at him. "Do you mean you didn't sleep last night?"

"I haven't slept in *eighteen months*." The way his mouth wraps around the words *eighteen months* makes me look harder at him. It's true. He looks like shit. He looks thin and pale and grief-stricken. The tension is thick in the air, making my heart beat hard. The baby kicks, her feet high up into my ribs, right under my hands. My belly squeezes again. Oh, my God. I'm having contractions.

I try my best not to let it show on my face. "It's hard to make decisions when you're not sleeping."

"When I try to sleep, all I see is that truck through the window. The headlights. Do you know what I'm talking about?"

I nod. "I do know. Dayton told me about it."

He barks out a laugh. "He admitted to you that he's a fucking murderer, and you're *still* with him?"

My palms go cold.

What the hell do I say to that?

I can deny that Day is a murderer. I can try to convince Alexei that it was an accident, a horrible accident. I can plead with him to see reason.

But I'm looking into the eyes of a man hollowed out with grief and rage, broken by loss and heartbreak, and I know there is nothing that I can say that will make any difference.

I shrug my shoulders, turning both palms up. "I love him," I say simply. "I can't walk away."

Alexei threads his hands through his hair and bends his forehead to the surface of the desk.

Then he looks up at me, his cold eyes red and empty. "He doesn't deserve that."

Another contraction comes down, squeezing the breath out of me. I don't want him to know that I'm in labor. I can't let him know. I know that as surely as I know that Dayton is coming for me.

Hold on.

Alexei stands up from the chair and stares down at me. "He doesn't deserve to walk around with you for the rest of his life." He shakes his head slowly. "I can't let him have that. Not after what he took from me."

"Let me tell you about some of the things we can offer you." I'm grasping at straws. There's nothing else left. At any moment now, Alexei could lift up his hoodie, take out the gun, and shoot me. "If you need a place to live, we have a place available. If you need to go to rehab, I have two standing by, ready to admit you. Have you ever thought about going to college, Alex? There are options for that, too."

His face goes blank, his gaze settling somewhere far away. "Kate was going to college."

"She was? Somewhere in the city?"

"Yeah." Alexei sticks his hands in his pockets. "Brooklyn College. I was taking extra jobs to pay for the tuition. She was going to go, then I was going to go, and then..."

I wait through another contraction. They're getting stronger. If my water breaks while I'm sitting here, I'm going to lose it.

"What happened?"

Alexei smiles, his face lighting up as if he's in the memory, pulled right back into the past. "Then she got pregnant. That baby—" He runs a hand through his hair again. "That baby was going to ruin all her plans, but we were so excited."

His eyes snap back to this reality.

"Oh, Alexei." I inject every bit of empathy I can into my voice. "I'm so sorry you lost your baby, and your wife. There just aren't any words."

With a strangled shout, he drops heavily back into the chair across from me. My pulse pounds in my ears. This is my final opening—I can sense it.

"You don't have to do this," I say softly. "There are other choices. If you want—" A contraction grips me, nearly stifling the words, but I force them out. "I'll help you."

"Oh, God." Alexei shudders and gets to his feet, horror lacing his eyes. "Fuck.'

He turns to face the office door and his shoulders drop.

"Alexei?"

"I don't have any choice now." His voice is empty, hollow. "I thought it was what I wanted, not to have any choice." He turns back and his eyes are resigned, committed. Panic swells into my gut at the same time as another contraction grips me. "And you don't have any choice, either."

42

DAYTON

THE CAB SCREECHES to a stop outside Heroes on the Home-front, and I shove myself out of the car so fast I barrel into a guy waiting on the curb. He starts to protest, takes one look at me, and asks Wes if we're done with the cab.

He waves him off. "—540 West Fiftieth," he says into his phone. "Potentially armed." He listens for a moment. "No." Then he hangs up.

"What the hell was that?"

"The police," he says simply. "That woman at the front desk hasn't called yet. Guy probably told her he'd kill everybody in there if she did."

"How long do we have?"

"Five minutes?"

Wes moves for the front door, turning when he realizes I'm still on the sidewalk. "Day? Get the fuck over here."

I open my mouth, then shut it again.

Wes rushes back, and I'm filled with shame for the precious seconds he has to waste doing whatever he's doing.

He looks me straight in the eye. "You belong here, asshole. You didn't bring this on her." He stabs a finger in the direction of the building. "That guy in there? Alex? He's the fucking sicko who decided to do this. You be there for her. Just like you've always been there for her, even if everybody said you were wrong."

"Fuck those people," I spit, even as the memories rise, even as I feel the Humvee lifting with the explosion, even as I feel the wheel of the drug-running car under my hands at the moment of impact.

Then we move toward the door together, like we're back in the unit, ready to face anything, together.

It's a scene.

Everyone who works in the office is crowded into the waiting room. Carla is sobbing at her desk, tears running silently down her face. I don't bother asking her anything. I head for Hazel, the one who's always bringing Summer doughnuts. She looks grim.

"They're still in there."

Hazel looks up at me, and I see the fear behind the stoic expression. "I can hear them talking when everybody shuts up."

Talking. Summer has him talking. That's my girl.

"Police are right behind us. You know what's going to happen if we can't get him out of there, right?"

She nods, once, then the meaning of the words hits her. "Day, you can't—" Wes is already at the entrance to the hallway. "Who's that?"

"Summer's brother."

Her hands fly to her hair. "Shit. You're going in there?"

"Right now. Get everybody out of the way."

I join Wes at the hall entrance and point down to the second door on the right. It's the only one that's closed.

Light on our feet, we take up positions on either side of the door. My breathing slows as my focus sharpens. I can hear Alexei's voice.

"—not to have any choice. And you don't have any choice, either."

"I'd say my options at this point are fairly limited," Summer answers. Her voice is steady, solemn. "All I can do is sit here. Look at me." There's a creak—she must be moving in her chair. "You, on the other hand—you still have choices."

"I don't."

"You *do*," she insists. "Let's start with the first one. You *don't* have to commit a crime here today."

"We're past that."

"We're having a meeting," she says lightly. "You think I haven't had meetings with a hundred men grieving for people they'll never get back?"

My heart twists in my chest. I never thought I'd get Summer back again. Never.

Wes moves in front of the door, his feet making no sound in the carpeted hallway. He locks eyes with me, pointing to both sets of hinges on the door. Then he points to his chest and mine. *Me or you first?*

I take a heartbeat to think about it. He's better trained. He's still in. He has to be the first one in that door, because he has the best chance at taking Alexei down.

Before I can answer, he points at his own chest again. *Me.*

"Why are you crying?" Alexei's question ends the planning phase. We're out of time.

We line ourselves up in front of the door, and in that moment, I'm back in Afghanistan, raiding a stronghold in the middle of the night, Wes at my side. Time slows. The hinges don't look very strong—they're brass, decorative. The carpet is tacky under my feet, new enough to have some grip to it.

Wes counts down on his fingers. *Three, two, one—*

The echo of his voice in the desert rings in my ears—*go, go, go*—and the door bursts open under the weight of our fury.

ALEXEI STARTLES and turns toward the door. He never gets the chance to face it completely. Wes rushes him, hooks an arm around his neck, and forces him down to his knees. "Where's the gun?" He shouts, forceful and demanding. "Where's the gun?" Wes isn't waiting for an answer. His arm tightens around Alexei's neck and his other hand searches him.

Alexei babbles something.

"Is there anything else, you fucker?"

Summer rises from her chair, tears and relief mixing on her face. Wes has Alexei under control—Alexei is sagging, his hands useless against Wes's arm.

"Day—" Summer puts her arms out and I kick away the chair behind her. I touch her face, her chin.

"Are you okay? Did he hurt you?"

"No." My hand still at her face, she turns her head sharply. "Wes. *Wes.*"

He's still moving around Alexei. He doesn't release his grip on him when he reaches to set something on the surface of Summer's desk, pointed away from all of us. A gun.

"You're going to kill him. He can't breathe." Summer's voice is steady, but she leans forward and braces herself with one palm on the edge of her desk. "*Wes.*"

He releases his grip on Alexei's neck and hauls him upright, pinning both arms behind his back. "What do you want me to do with him?" Wes addresses the question to the room as if there's a committee waiting to decide. Alexei hangs his head.

"Alex." I put one hand on Summer's back. Alexei looks up at me. He's a ruined man. "I'm sorry about Kate. I should never have agreed to drive you anywhere that night."

His expression is pure anguish. "She was pregnant."

It's not an explanation. In this moment, there's no need for an explanation. It was only a trick of fate that took Kate from him and gave Summer back to me. My rage bleeds out of me.

"The police are about to get here. Wes—"

"You're fucking kidding me." His eyes are hard with skepticism. "They can have him."

"They can't," Summer says. "He didn't shoot anyone. I never saw the gun. He needs *help*, Wes. Get him help."

Everybody in the room looks at her. I stroke her hair. "Sunny—"

"He needs help," she repeats. "So if you're not going to let him get that, then—"

"Just kill me now." Alexei says the words through gritted teeth. "Just fucking kill me now."

Summer shakes her head. "See? This isn't—" She blows a stiff breath out through rounded lips and bows her head, knuckles going white on the edge of the desk.

"Sunny?" My heart punches like a fist against my ribcage. "Are you sure he didn't hurt you? Here, sit down, sit—"

On the next breath, she straightens up. "I'm *fine*," she says, putting both hands to the small of her back. "Except—the baby's coming. Right now."

43

I'm not entirely right.

Dayton and Wes realize what's happening at the same time, and both talk over one another as Dayton rushes me toward the door, as fast and delicately as he can.

The police are at the end of the hall.

"We have a man in crisis," I say to the first one. "He is in *crisis*. He needs mental health services *now*." I look the officer in the eye. "Do you hear me?"

His partner is already racing into my office. "Ma'am, I'm going to need you to—"

"Alexei Sokolov is the one in crisis in the office," Day says. "But this woman is in labor. She can't give a statement right now."

The cop's eyes go wide, and he steps out of the way as another contraction hits.

"Shit, Day," I whisper under my breath. He puts an arm

around what's left of my waist and gives me something to lean on. This is *not* how I imagined the labor process would go. It wasn't exactly on my bucket list to have a contraction in front of everyone in the entire office, much less during a hostage situation, so this is all excellent. Just excellent.

When the contraction subsides, we get through the waiting area and outside. Day steps off the curb and waves down a yellow cab. It pulls up to the curb, and I'm gripped with the need to stay outside of it. The heat cracks like an egg on top of my head and sweat drips down over every inch of my skin. No, no, *no*. If it's this hot outside, it's going to be worse in the cab. I need to be free.

"Come on, Sunny. It's time to go to the hospital."

"I don't want to get in the cab."

Day waves his hand inside the door. "It's got air conditioning. It's nice in there."

"I don't want to sit down."

"You've got to. Just for a few minutes. Okay?" He comes back and takes my face in his hands. "Sunny, you can't have the baby on the sidewalk."

Out of the corner of my eye, I see Wes run out of Heroes on the Homefront. "Were you guys leaving without me?" There's a shake in his voice that everyone ignores.

"I don't want to get in the cab."

They exchange a look over my head.

"I hate when you do that," I snarl. "I've always hated when you do that. Look at each other like I'm some little kid, and you're going to do whatever you want. It's the fucking—" My voice is choked off by a contraction that hits me with the force of a tsunami. It shuts everything down in my brain, drilling my focus down to the pressure.

"Ready?" Wes says it like he's said it a million times, and all the memories flash into my mind. *Ready* at the back door of the house, at the top of the sledding hill, at the beginning of a game.

Dayton takes my other arm. "Go."

They pick me up and place me in the cab between them, and through the haze of pain, I hear Day giving the address of the hospital to the cab driver. "Fast," he says to the driver. I lift my head to see his eyes reflected in the rearview mirror. They look concerned. I know what *that's* about.

"Your car's going to be fine," I shout.

I have three more contractions in the car. By the time we reach the hospital, the intensity of each one is way over my head, blurring out everything else.

For the first time in my life, I feel trapped inside my own body. The contractions are so strong, it's like a vise around my belly, and holy *shit*, it hurts. When they let up, the relief is so sweet.

And so short.

I am caught in a series of animal needs. I refuse the wheel-chair on the way to labor and delivery.

"Are you sure? Sunny, it's just—"

"I'm not sitting down," I thunder at Day, and he exchanges a look with the nurse who's there with the chair.

"It's not far," she says.

It might as well be a hundred miles.

I brace against the wall with every contraction, leaning into it.

Day is always with me, his hands on my lower back, on my hips. Voices blend with one another. A nurse shows him how to give me counter-pressure, and he does. He must be the only one strong enough to do it. He *is* the only one strong enough to stand with me through this.

He's the only one I've ever wanted.

In the delivery room, his hands work at my clothes even as I shout at him to get them off of me. The maternity tank I loved so much feels like rubber against my skin. I'm hot. I'm so hot.

My water breaks, gushing onto the floor beneath me, and everything intensifies. I thought it was bad before, but this is hell. I cannot get away from my own body, but even if I could, I'd never want to be away from him.

Or the baby.

The only way I can survive this is on my hands and knees. Day sits on the bed and I press my head into his chest with each howling contraction. The smell of him is my only comfort.

"Lay down," he says softly, during one of those islands of peace. "Lay down, Sunny."

"Why?" I don't want to.

"You have no choice, sweetheart."

He moves out of the way and helps me turn. "Ten centimeters," says one of the nurses, her voice cool, a soothing balm. The next contraction comes down hard. Someone in the room is screaming.

"It's time to push, honey," says the nurse from the foot of the bed. "That's it. That's it. Ten—nine—eight—" The numbers trip over one another in my mind. She turns to look over her shoulder. There are other people in the room, people I've not noticed before, people pulling down a warming bed and unwrapping tools, people preparing in a hurry.

I need something to hold onto.

I need something—

Day takes my hand. I blink and the red at the edges of my vision clears. "You're tough, Sunny. You're doing this."

"It *hurts*," I tell him.

"You're the toughest girl in the world," he says.

"One more push," says the nurse. "One, two, three."

44

"You're still here."

Wes shifts in the waiting room chair and blinks. "Wasn't asleep. I was on guard," he mumbles, and then his eyes open wide. "Holy shit. Holy *shit*, Day, there she is." His voice is filled with wonder and sleep. He jumps up from the chair and shakes himself out. He's still wearing the same t-shirt and jeans as before. Somehow, it surprises me. It seems like we've been here forever.

"Here she fucking is, man."

My daughter.

She is here in my arms, fresh and soft and recently bathed. Her tiny, pink face is creased as if she's been sleeping for a long time. She's sleeping now, in my arms, swaddled in hospital blankets with baby footprint patterns. As I watch her—as we *both* watch her—her mouth squeezes into a pout and then relaxes again.

Wes clears his throat. "Is—is everything cool? That guy from the office isn't going to come bursting in here, is he?" There's a tired worry in his eyes.

"No. Summer's office called a little while ago. They arranged to get him admitted at a place. I guess he was a suicide risk." I don't want to think about Alexei, but even Summer asked about him. These Sullivans. "The police are going to be keeping an eye on him for a long time."

"Good. That's good." Wes smiles down at the baby. "She's safe, then."

"Do you want to hold her?"

He smiles, making a small *ttt* sound with his tongue. "You think I should?" He puts a hand to the back of his neck. "Mom's going to be pissed I got to hold her first."

"You can tell her *I* got to hold her first. Throw me under the bus. I don't care."

"Okay. Should I—" He motions to the chair.

I give him a look. "You can do this standing up."

"All right. All right."

I lean in close and transfer her gently into his waiting arms. "Support her neck."

"I *know*." He looks down into her face and his eyebrows rise. "Wow," he says softly.

"I *know*."

All of me is aching from the lack of adrenaline, and that's probably what makes me so fucking sappy. But my chest warms at the sight of him in this waiting room. He didn't have to wait here. He didn't have to walk back into my life at all. But sometimes the past has a tight grip.

"So—" He moves from side to side a little. "Is everything okay?"

"Yeah. Yeah." I'm suddenly bereft without the little weight of her in my arms, so I stick my hands in my pocket. "She's a month early, so they were worried she might not be, you know, ready to be on the outside, but everything's fine. She's a little on the petite side. Six pounds even."

"That's good." Wes flicks his eyes back to me. "And Sunny?"

"Sleeping."

Wes laughs quietly. "I was going to go in and give her a high-five, but—"

"Another time."

"Another time," he agrees. Then he looks at me, waiting.

"What?"

"Dude." He turns his attention back to the most precious thing that exists on the planet. "What's her name?"

I can't stop the ridiculous grin. "January."

"You're shitting me," he says, so gently I stifle my laugh with my hand.

"No. It was Summer's idea."

"A winter baby born when it's hotter than blazes." Wes is incredulous. "You *would* do that."

I think of how brave Summer's been all day. One thing after another. Alexei. The baby coming early. Those moments of fear when she was first born, when we didn't know if she was going to spend any time in the NICU. "It's true. I'd let her get away with murder."

"Why January? Why not September?"

Summer's eyes, blue in the dim light of the delivery room, shining with pride and exhaustion. "She said January was when the *before* was finally over."

Wes looks to the side, eyes crinkling. "I don't think I need to hear any more about that."

We stand in a comfortable silence. He looks down at January, who stirs lightly in his arms and settles back to sleep. I'm still shaken up by how different everything is now. A few hours ago, she was a figure of speech, a future plan, and now she's *here,* shifting the gravity of the earth. How can someone so small change the way the planet spins? I don't know, but she's doing it.

I never imagined that Wes would be here for this. Not in my wildest dreams. For years, I've thought that even if we ran into each other, it would all be broken. I blink hard. No. This is real. We're here in this empty waiting room in the middle of the night, both of us still alive.

"I missed you, man."

He looks at me, then back down at January. "I don't like admitting this kind of shit, but I missed you, too."

I laugh.

"You turned out okay without me."

"That's the thing." January fusses and he stands up, tense. I take my hands out of my pockets and accept her back into my arms. She turns her face to my shirt and nuzzles, her mouth puckered in a baby frown. Then, just like that, the storm has passed. She curls up again and I stroke her forehead. "I'm better *with* you around. I know, it seems—stop laughing, you ass—it seems stupid, but I need you in my life. This little girl's going to need you, too."

Wes nods, looking down at the bundle in my arms. "Shit, man."

Then he steps forward and puts one arm around my shoulders, patting my back, being extra careful not to crowd the baby.

"Mr. Nash?"

Wes steps back and shoves his hands into his pockets, blinking fast.

"Yeah?"

One of the nurses has poked her head into the door of the waiting room. "Summer's asking for you."

"I gotta go. You should go, too. Get some sleep."

Wes looks at me with a crooked grin. "Congratulations, man."

He leads the way out of the waiting room, then heads to the right. Summer's room is down to the left. I watch him walk away, his head held high. A little way down the hall, he raises one fist in the air, a silent celebration.

"Hey," I call after him. He stops, turning on his heel. "You coming back tomorrow?"

"It'll be a fucking madhouse. My parents—" He rolls his eyes.

"Be here," I tell him.

"I'll be here."

45

I WAKE UP TO SINGING.

For a long while, I don't want to open my eyes. I can't. I'm pinned down by how utterly wrung out I feel. Every muscle aches. It'll be time again for painkillers soon, I hope.

Then I focus in again on the singing. It's Dayton.

I stretch out under the hospital sheets, inch by inch. I feel accomplished. And...empty. His voice is so sweet and soft. I can hardly make out the words. A few, here and there, and then I recognize it.

"—before I met you," he sings, then starts humming the tune.

I open my eyes.

He's in the rocker facing the window, January in his arms. Both of them are bathed in the creamy gray light of early morning. My eyes well with tears at the sight of them.

I gingerly push myself up on one elbow, and Day stops humming and turns. "Hey, gorgeous."

I groan. "I am a *wreck*."

He stands up and comes over to the bed, and I make room. It's not a very wide bed, so I'm right up against the plastic railing, but I don't care. The line of his body against mine, even in his jeans and t-shirt, makes me feel a thousand times better.

"You're not a wreck." I hold out my arms for January and he puts her tenderly into my arms. It's the most natural thing I've ever done, holding her. I was afraid, at odd moments during the pregnancy, that I wouldn't know what to do when she was born. But when they put her on my chest for the first time, everything changed. "You made this wonder of a person."

"We did." A glow of pride sweeps over me. Then the ache sets in again. "What time is it?"

"Just after five." He seems to read my mind. "They'll be back at five-thirty with your next round of painkillers."

"Thank God."

Day curls his arm around me and pulls us both in close. "Is it bad?"

I think about it. "It's pretty bad," I admit. "But all things considered, I'd do it again."

He laughs out loud and January startles. "Don't tempt me."

"I'm not. I'm *definitely* not." He bends to kiss my cheek. "Not yet, at least."

Day reaches over to the bedside table for something. "Did you see these?" It's a thin stack of papers. "We have to fill out the information for her birth certificate and social security card."

"*That's* official."

He scans through the papers. "Think we should do it now?"

"You got anything better to do?"

Dayton grins. "No." He grabs a pen from the bedside table. "They even left a clipboard." He lines up the papers on the clipboard, uncaps the pen, and then takes a deep breath. "You sure about January?"

"It's her name," I say, my throat tightening. God, this is going to be a *ride,* if even talking about her name makes me choked up. "I'm sure of it. January." As if she recognizes the name, she opens her eyes and stretches, raising her tiny fists above her head, which is covered in a pink knitted hat. Day stops writing to look at her, and as he does, she opens her mouth and squalls. The sound makes my heart race. "Oh, baby, it's all right. It's all right." I clasp her to me, her cries seeming to get louder every second. "It's all right…"

"Maybe she's hungry," Dayton hints, and it brings me back to reality.

"Right." I laugh a little, the nervousness draining away. Conveniently, my hospital gown has snaps up at the top. I pop them open and pull down the cotton tank top Day bought me at the little gift shop downstairs. It's not *ideal,* but it'll do until we have a chance to get some other things. January wails up to the moment she latches on, then settles. I stare down at her. "Is that—do you think that's right?"

"Looks right to me," Day says. "Looks *more* than right." The faintest hint of desire in his voice makes me meet his eyes. They're shining.

"Are you *hitting* on me in the hospital?" I say, my voice rising.

He raises both hands in the air. "I can't help it. No, that's not true. I'll help it."

"Don't help it," I tell him. I do not feel desirable right now, but in his eyes, I see hope for the future.

"Okay." He focuses back on the paperwork and writes *January* in clear block letters. The pen hovers over the space for her last name.

I wait.

"Are you going to write it?"

He gives me a sidelong look. "I'm...not exactly sure what to write."

"We talked about this, didn't we?"

Dayton shakes his head and presses his lips together like he's carefully reading every line of what has to be the easiest form on the planet. "I think we planned to talk about it, but we never actually did." His right foot jiggles near the end of the bed. Is he *nervous*?

"Nash," I say simply. "That's her last name."

His eyes go wide. "Are you sure about that?" He takes a deep breath. "That's a big deal, Sunny. That's—" Day sits up straight. "I don't want to mess this up. He laughs a little. "The form, I mean. So if you're not sure—"

"Day."

"Yeah?"

"I'm sure about *you*. I waited for you for a decade. And every single one of those years was worth it."

He looks faux-offended. "Only a decade?"

"I'd wait a thousand years if it meant being with you." I'm deadly serious, on the verge of tears. Giving birth, it turns out, is no joke.

Dayton softens. "Sunny, I'd wait forever." He leans in and kisses me. All the pain melts away under the possessive softness of his lips.

When we resurface, I look him in the eye. "Write it."

He writes down her last name. *His* last name. Someday soon, it'll be my last name, too. I've already decided.

"So," he says, beaming. "Is this a good time to propose?"

"No way," I tell him. "I want to at least have washed my hair. And—wait!"

"What?"

It was supposed to be a surprise. I was going to pop the question when he wasn't expecting it. I think he's forgotten about the ring—the bag from the jewelry store has been collecting dust on our kitchen counter ever since. "Nothing. Nothing. Don't worry about it."

A nurse knocks on the door and pushes her way in carrying a meal tray. "I hope I'm not interrupting anything," she says, startlingly chipper for this early in the morning.

"Only the best day of our lives," Dayton answers, and he means every word.

46

Two Weeks Later

SHE'S GONE.

I know, because the first thing I do when I wake up is feel for her on the other side of the bed. The sheets are cold. Summer's not here.

I sit up and rub my hands over my face. What time is it? Ungodly o'clock, that's what. January hasn't settled into a routine yet, and it's slowly killing the both of us. "Wait two weeks and she'll be a different baby," Summer's mother told us in the hospital that first day. "If anything's tough, wait two weeks."

I hear her.

I hear the imprint of soft footsteps in the other room, the gentle creak of the floorboards. How long has she been awake?

I throw my legs over the side of the bed and tug on my prosthetic. It's still hot, mid-September, and the air-conditioning unit we've got running in the bedroom is hardly touching the heat. Still, I appreciate that it's trying as I pass by in front of it.

In the doorway of the bedroom, I pause.

Summer is at the end of the hall, pacing back and forth. She's wearing panties and a nursing tank, one side unclipped. Her blonde hair is spilling out of the bun it's tied back in. I can tell by the way she's walking that she's been up for hours, letting me sleep.

God, I love her so much.

Now's the time.

I go back into the bedroom and open the top drawer of the dresser. It takes maneuvering around a bunch of boxers and nursing bras to get to it, but there it is, in the back left corner —a small velvet box. I take the ring out and slip it onto my pinky finger.

In the living room, Summer is over by the window, speaking softly to January. "It's all right to rest, sweetheart. You can go to sleep. I know it's dark out, but we're all here, and you don't have to stay awake anymore. Go to sleep, go to sleep..." I step on one of the old creaky floorboards and she turns her head. There are dark circles under her eyes. She's stressed. She hasn't slept, clearly. "Day."

I plant a kiss on her forehead and take January from her arms, standing straight and tall. There's no pain in my leg at all, or anywhere else. Being a little tired? I can handle that.

Summer stretches her elbows over her head, then holds out her hands for the baby.

"Are you kidding?" I laugh softly, swaying from side to side. In my arms, January blinks slowly, her eyes fluttering. "I've got this. Go to sleep."

"Are you sure?" Her face is a picture of concern. "What if—"

"If she gets hungry, I'll bring her to you. Go to sleep. Sleep as long as you want."

"Dayton—"

"Sunny." She rubs the back of her hand across her eyes. "You know you can count on me for this, right? For everything?"

"I know." Summer rises on tiptoes and kisses my cheekbone. Relief radiates off her. She's been trying so hard to make this easy on *me*. I'm going to out-do her. She steps around me, heading for the hallway.

"Sunny?"

"Yeah?" She comes back a few steps, eyebrows knitted together with worry. "Do you need something before I go? I can get you a blanket, or—"

I clear my throat. "I wanted you to know something. That's all."

"What?" Sunny stands in front of me, rocking back and forth like she's still holding January.

"What I mean is that you can count on me always. Forever." I slip the ring off my pinky finger and hold it out to her with my free hand. In my arms, January coos once and closes her eyes. "I'd get down on one knee, but she's *just* falling asleep..." Summer squints at the ring and I laugh a little. "Marry me."

Her face lights up. "Yes."

"That doesn't sound very enthusiastic."

"The baby *just* fell asleep," she says, a warning tone in her voice.

"I won't wake her up." I lean down to kiss Summer, the warm bundle between us sound asleep.

Summer pulls back abruptly. "Wait."

"What?"

"Wait here."

She dashes for the kitchen counter. There's a rustle of a paper bag, and she's back in a few moments, holding out a ring. A ring we picked out what seems like a million years ago. "Dayton," she says, voice trembling. "Will you marry me?"

It's a sheer joy, having her ask me that question. I'll never tell her how much I like it. "Fucking A, Sunny, I thought you'd never propose."

"Shh!" She scolds me with the lightest frown. "Watch your language. Our daughter hears everything you say."

"Sorry."

We both lean down, one by one, to kiss January's forehead. Her skin is *so* soft. Summer slips my ring onto my finger and lifts her face to mine. A few heartbeats in and the heat in the kiss is growing, *growing*—

She pulls back, putting her fingertips to her lips as if they've been burned.

"I had a baby *two* weeks ago." Summer waves a finger at me. "Cool your jets."

"You know," I tell her, keeping my voice even and soft, not daring to wake the baby, not daring to take another moment of precious sleep from Summer. "Before you were mine, I never would have—"

"Before?" She laughs, the sound low and sensual. "There was no *before*. I've *always* been yours."

EPILOGUE
SUMMER

My wedding day was supposed to go off without a hitch.

For one thing, it's a spring wedding, which means we *had* to have it inside. You can't predict the weather in April, so my mom didn't get the big outdoor gala that she wanted. We settled on a reception hall in the city that has huge windows, though. *Everything* is flooded with natural light. Weather? No problem.

I didn't count on the teething.

January is seven months old and an absolute wreck.

Five days ago—yes, *five days ago*—she started fussing. I had no idea why. No matter what I did, she fussed and fussed and fussed, until finally Dayton snapped. He came home from work and took her to the pediatrician. When I got home, he was sitting there with a perfectly healthy baby.

"What'd they do?" I asked him, wonderingly.

"Told me to give her some Tylenol. She's teething." He smiles, rolling his eyes.

AMELIA WILDE

"*Teething*? She's only seven months old?"

He'd pulled me into his arms and kissed me. "What, did you think she'd wait until she's two?"

"No. But the *wedding*—"

"Tylenol," he said firmly.

The thing about Tylenol is that it only works if you *give it to the baby.* My parents did a nice thing for us last night and took January to their house so we could finalize some last minute wedding details and, shall we say, *work out our frustrations.* It was perfect.

Until my mother delivered a cranky baby to me who'd already drooled through her back-up outfit.

It's fine, really. January is clad only in a diaper, since I'm not putting on her fancy dress until the last moment, and we're still waiting for the emergency Tylenol to kick in. She's *so* uncomfortable that I don't want to put her down. That should only make it slightly more difficult when it comes time to put on my dress.

The stylist looks at us both in the mirror. "Can you tilt your chin up a bit, honey?"

I tilt my chin up and try my best to watch January in the mirror. She's calming a bit, leaning back in my arms and gnawing at a teether shaped like a strawberry. She catches sight of me in the mirror and smiles a big, gummy grin that warms my heart.

"Hi, boo boo," I tell her in the glass, and the stylist laughs.

Hitch over.

Except—

"It's quiet in here." I look around at the bridal suite as much as I can without moving my head. "Where's my mom?"

"She probably went to get another glass of wine from the caterer," the stylist says. "Helps to calm the nerves."

"What nerves?" Everybody else is made up, dresses on. I'm the last to get my hair done. Then we have half an hour for pictures before the ceremony. How did the morning go by so *fast?*

I entertain January, playing little games with the teether, and then the stylist is done. "How's that?"

"Honestly, I'm a vision." It's true—my makeup is flawless. My hair is on point. This is happening. The solid weight of January in my arms is all that's grounding me. Today is the day I marry the love of my life. *Today.*

The doors to the bridal suite burst open. In the mirror, I see my mother and turn to face her, standing up with January in my arms. "Thank God, Mom! We've got to get me in this dress." She's followed closely behind by my maid of honor, Whitney—"*obviously*," she'd say if you asked her about it— and Hazel, who still works with me at Heroes on the Home-front and is thrilled to be a bridesmaid. The three of them exchange a look.

"Oh, no," I say, trying to keep my smile in place. Trying to keep my *cool* in place. "What's the look for?"

My mom opens her mouth and shuts it again, eyes welling with tears.

"Mom? Did something happen?"

"You—" She presses her lips together and shakes her head. "You look absolutely gorgeous, Sunny."

"Thanks, Mom, really." I can't help glowing with a little bit of pride. All of this has been crazy to put together with a new baby and both of us working. I'm surprised we pulled it off.

Or maybe we haven't.

"There's a slight issue," Whitney says. "With your brother."

"With Wes?" I rack my brain for any possible issue he could be having. He came to the city a few days ago for Day's bachelor party, said he had some things to do, and checked into the hotel attached to the reception hall. Day hasn't texted me about anything going wrong this morning, but— "What's wrong with Wes?" He's the best man. He's got the rings. He knows where he has to be.

"We can't find him."

AUTHOR'S NOTE

Our hero Dayton Nash is a creation of my imagination, but his struggles with PTSD reflect reality for many veterans and servicemembers. One of readers suggested that I include information about the Veterans Crisis Line here for anyone who might need it—endless thanks to you, Ramona.

If you are a veteran or servicemember in crisis, or are the friend or loved one of a veteran or servicemember in crisis, please consider contacting the Veterans Crisis Line. They are available 24 hours a day, 7 days a week, 365 days a year via phone, online chat, or text.

Call 1-800-273-8255 (Press 1)
Send a text to 838255
Chat at veteranscrisisline.net

For more books by Amelia Wilde, visit her online at
www.awilderomance.com

Made in the USA
Coppell, TX
06 June 2022